A Tale

MAHARSHI PATEL is a first-generation immigrant currently living in the United States. He was born in India, did his elementary school in England, and has lived in various states in the US before settling in Charlotte, North Carolina. He is a proud alumnus of Duke University. It was during a five-month journey back to his roots in Ahmedabad that he was inspired to write this story about two generations split by more than miles.

A Tale
of
Two Indians

Maharshi Patel

Ashley,

To an awesome work buddy!

- Maharshi

HARPER

VANTAGE

First published in India in 2011 by Harper Vantage
An imprint of HarperCollins *Publishers* India
a joint venture with
The India Today Group

Copyright © Maharshi Patel 2011

ISBN: 978-93-5029-115-3

2 4 6 8 10 9 7 5 3 1

Maharshi Patel asserts the moral right
to be identified as the author of this work

This is a work of fiction and all characters and incidents described in this book are
the product of the author's imagination. Any resemblance to actual persons,
living or dead, is entirely coincidental.

All rights reserved. No part of this publication may be reproduced,
stored in a retrieval system, or transmitted, in any form or by any means,
electronic, mechanical, photocopying, recording or otherwise,
without the prior permission of the publishers.

HarperCollins *Publishers*
A-53, Sector 57, Noida 201301, India
77-85 Fulham Palace Road, London W6 8JB, United Kingdom
Hazelton Lanes, 55 Avenue Road, Suite 2900, Toronto, Ontario M5R 3L2
and 1995 Markham Road, Scarborough, Ontario M1B 5M8, Canada
25 Ryde Road, Pymble, Sydney, NSW 2073, Australia
31 View Road, Glenfield, Auckland 10, New Zealand
10 East 53rd Street, New York NY 10022, USA

Typeset in 11/14 Adobe Caslon Pro
InoSoft Systems

Printed and bound at
Thomson Press (India) Ltd.

This book is dedicated to everyone who lent me a hand when I was down. Without your help, I would never have been able to stand up again.

Contents

The Darkest Hour . . .

'Life begins on the other side of despair.' – Jean-Paul Sartre

As the rays of the afternoon sun hit his face, his sleepy eyes involuntarily jerked open. The feather-soft bed and the Egyptian satin sheets that were caressing his body made it a little difficult for him to getup. His head was still pounding from having stayed up till dawn. He fumbled about for his wristwatch and saw that it was one in the afternoon. With a groan, Maharshi Patel pulled himself awake.

He lumbered into the bathroom and looked at himself in the mirror. His once attractive 6' 3" frame reflected back. His chocolate-brown eyes that used to be aflame with arrogant self-confidence now appeared downcast and ashamed. While his skin had retained its fair complexion, a thick stubble had grown over his perennially clean-shaven face. The jet-black hair that he kept neatly combed was tousled. Dandruff fell like snowflakes from his hair when he shook his head and looked down. Like Lucifer, his proud and noble features had been exchanged for the irreverent rage and wild state of a fallen angel. On the floor he spotted the Versace sunglasses that he had violently thrown aside in frustration lastnight; he looked with detachment at his Lacoste shirt and Ralph Lauren khakis, witnesses to the changes that had overtaken their teenaged wearer.

Maharshi staggered back to his bedroom and sat at his desk, sinking into a luxurious leather executive office chair. And the previous night revisited him in all its fury.

'What are you doing with your life, Maharshi? You've failed us, you've failed your entire family, and you've failed yourself!'

That line had come from his father.

'Have you lost your mind? Did you think that no one would ever find out?'

That was his mother.

'We should never have even sent him to college; tossing a hundred and fifty thousand dollars into a drain would have been a better investment.'

He couldn't really remember who had said that.

The yells, the screams, the tears all came back to Maharshi. His parents telling him that he was an abject failure in all his ambitions. His thinking that there was no way out of his predicament, deciding that it would be better for him to just die rather than suffer the agonies of an unfair world. Secretly grabbing the keys to his S500 Mercedes Benz and running for the garage, trying to race out, his mother jumping in front of the car and stopping him from executing his desperate plan . . . .

He couldn't bear the flashbacks any more. Popping three Tylenols to ease his throbbing head, Maharshi walked downstairs. His eyes went over the luxuries surrounding the $1.2 million mansion. He glanced outside as he descended the stairs: the large glass windows offered him a view of massive Corinthian pillars that stood proudly over the majestic entrance. He lingered for a moment as he passed the parlour and, with a glum eye, observed the oriental silk settees, the elegant drapes adorning the windows, the handmade stained-glass lamps. He looked at the many framed pictures around the house, and grimaced. There were photos of him in happier times: standing upright in a fitted tuxedo during a prom night, playing and laughing in the snow in Switzerland, posing next to a lion in Gir forest. Seeing the picture from his cousin's wedding, in which he was wearing a designer silk kurta, Maharshi vaguely remembered a family friend commenting that he looked like a maharaja from the colonial days.

Maharshi grimaced again and moved on, past the mahogany dining table and its lion-foot, silk-backed chairs; the tall lighted statue of two flamingoes that decorated the hallway; and the papyrus painting on the wall. He looked up and saw the rarely used Bose speaker system that had been installed just a month ago. He crossed the living room with its sumptuous Italian leather sofas and ultra-modern glass coffee table, he passed the door that led to his basement and the 110-inch indoor movie theatre contained within, built especially for him. At the fully stocked wine bar he spotted the two empty bottles of Dom Perignon his father had opened just a week before.

His cell phone vibrated in his pocket. A new text message.

'Dinner@the country club?'

The words barely registered in Maharshi's mind. It seemed as if a lifetime had passed since he last went to the country club, even though it had only been a few days. He deleted the message and went into the kitchen.

Maharshi made himself a mug of coffee and sat at the black granite island, easing into a leather bar stool. He soon became restless and stepped outside. He saw people playing out on the fourteenth fairway of the golf course that his mansion was set upon. The seated Buddha atop the artificial waterfall seemed to be winking at him knowingly. The imported palms and the many exotic flowers that garlanded the waterfall made the landscape appear like a small slice of tropical rainforest. Maharshi sat on one of the rarely used benches next to it and tried, with as much calm as he could muster, to listen to the tranquil sound of the flowing water. He glanced down and his eyes fell on the half-carat diamond, set in platinum and gold, that adorned his ring finger.

The coffee was too hot. He decided to set it aside and closed his eyes.

Maharshi wondered what had led him to this depth of despair. Hell, he had even intended to drive to an unknown oblivion in a Mercedes. What on earth could have pushed a young man with a life as luxurious as his into wanting everything to fade?

Life hadn't always been like this for Maharshi Kashyap Patel. In fact, for the first fourteen years of his life, he had no real place to call home. He was born in Ahmedabad. His father had left for England when he was three and Maharshi had joined him there a year later with his mother. They changed houses every six months, and he invariably lost any friends he made during the short stays. After many moves, they finally came to America. Maharshi stayed in small rented apartments with only his mother for company, as Kashyap worked day and night. He wore old clothes and played with toys that were bought second-hand from garage sales.

And yet, despite the spartan lifestyle, despite the short-lived friendships, despite the frequent moves, Maharshi was happy. He had loving parents. He could watch *Power Rangers* and *The Jungle Book* enveloped in his mother's warm arms every night. He was so morally righteous that Kashyap nicknamed him 'Little Gandhi'. He felt uncomfortable lying even to telemarketers about his parents being home; and he would always insist that his father be on the right side of the law, even in matters such as speed limits and seatbelts.

In America, Maharshi's family first shared a home with his maternal uncle Tushar in New Jersey, while Kashyap had his residency in New York. When the time came to move to Philadelphia for his father's fellowship, the young boy was inconsolable. His father tried bribing him with the fact that he would now have his own room. Maharshi screamed that he would rather live in a tiny hut with his whole family than have his own room and be separated from his aunt and uncle. The move went through nonetheless, and eventually he recovered.

In Philadelphia, Maharshi began to show signs of remarkable intelligence. He was selected to qualify for a programme for gifted students run by Johns Hopkins University, for which he had to take the SAT college admissions exam while in the eighth grade. He scored 1320, at the age of thirteen, much higher than the average score of most college-bound American teenagers. He won a scholarship for his efforts.

Finally, after Kashyap finished his fellowship, they moved to Charlotte, North Carolina, where he began practising oncology.

That is when his life began to change.

And also when Maharshi began to change.

Kashyap's practice expanded rapidly. Before Maharshi could fathom it, his father had become the most successful oncologist in the Carolinas and his name had become nationally renowned.

He remembered the conversation as if it had happened just the day before, even though it had taken place during winter break in eleventh grade.

His parents had come home from work early that day.

'Maharshi, hurry up and get dressed. We're going to have dinner at Zebra tonight.'

'You have a reservation, Dad?'

'Obviously. Why else would I be telling you? Wear something nice.'

Maharshi had only been to the 4 diamond French restaurant once before, when it was on the tab of a pharmaceutical company.

Over frozen soufflé with Grand Marnier, his dad dropped the bombshell.

'Son, your uncle and I finally finished reimbursements today.'

For the last six months, his father had been slaving day and night with the help of his maternal uncle to start a new practice. Kashyap and Jim Welsh, a fellow partner, were going through an acrimonious splitting from the managing partner. Needless to say, it meant hell for the family. Maharshi was glad that it was finally over and the reimbursements had come out.

Kashyap had a knowing smile and continued, 'Take a guess as to how much we made this year, Son.'

'$200,000?' Kashyap had often discussed what kind of money he expected once the messes of clinic finances were sorted out.

'Little higher.'

'$250,000?'

'Still a little higher.'

'$300,000?'

'Getting closer but not there. This is just the beginning. We've just entered the penthouse suite.'

From that day onwards, Maharshi's lifestyle took a huge upward swing. They bought the mansion on the golf course. Maharshi received a Mercedes Benz as his first car, as his tastes rose exponentially. Suddenly, he started desiring the best, and he got it.

Maharshi's grades didn't suffer; in fact, they improved if anything. He scored a perfect verbal and near-perfect math score on his SAT exams and gained admission to Duke University, one of the most prestigious colleges in the country, while also being the winner of the $5,000 Cameron Morrison scholarship to the University of North Carolina at Chapel Hill, and was a finalist for the National Merit Scholarship.

Maharshi's achievements boosted his ego, and the decadent materialism around him drove it up even more. Designer clothes, five-star restaurants, and soaking in Jacuzzis rapidly became his style. Regularly partying with his shallow friends, he soon started living a life of hedonism and ease with pleasure being his life's only goal. He complained that he only had a silver spoon and was constantly trying to trade it for one made of gold. A Rolex on his wrist and a Bentley in the garage became his immediate mission. The scion of two loving and rich parents, Maharshi led the perfect life, one that was envied by many and lived by a precious few. He forgot all about his early hardship, and the self-indulgence made him a different person.

This was not the man Maharshi had been raised to be. Kashyap had always tried to teach him that happiness didn't come from material wealth but from following the path of truth and morality. When he was a little boy, Maharshi had lived by that mantra and believed it to be entirely true. But by the time he went to college, he had forgotten the values he had imbibed from his father.

Then, one cold afternoon in February 2008 started a series of events in Maharshi's life that would culminate in the terrible events of that night in May 2009.

Maharshi had just stepped out of his dorm at Duke. The sky had shrouded the landscape and the Gothic-style university with a dark veil. There was a bitter chill in the air. The branches on the leafless trees were swaying gloomily. The freezing wind stabbed through the layers of Maharshi's Lacoste jacket like a blade, but did nothing to dull his excitement. He was waiting for his father who had called him earlier to tell him that he had just bought a new Lexus and was driving up to show it to him.

Kashyap arrived a few minutes later. Two of his friends were also in the car. Maharshi noted that it was odd for his father's friends to accompany him on a 200-mile drive, the sole purpose of which was to show him a new car. Even odder was their nervous demeanour. Maharshi got into the car and instantly sensed the tension. But he didn't say anything. They drove around for a bit, then came back to his dorm. After the perfunctory questions of how classes were going and how his friends were doing, Kashyap beckoned him to take a seat and slowly began to speak.

'Beta, I got a call from your mother in India. Jyoti Ba . . . passed away yesterday afternoon.'

Maharshi had spent most of his formative years with his grandmother in India. On the day that he moved into Duke to begin freshman year, she had been diagnosed with cancer. Maharshi wasn't informed until he went back home for the winter break six months later. She had responded well to chemotherapy in the meantime and was well on the way to recovery by the time Maharshi found out. That was when she had surgery for her hernia. Her intestines, already weakened by radiation therapy, weren't strong enough to handle the procedure. Two holes were punched in her duodenum.

Maharshi had gone to visit her during his winter vacation. Despite being warned ahead of time, he couldn't part with the mental image he still had from his memories with her. He recollected how her face lit up when she set eyes on him as he first walked though her door every time he visited. He fondly remembered how she used to hurry into the kitchen to emerge with his favourite piping-hot dishes, and never allowed him to stop eating until he had finished everything. She told him stories of his antics with her when he was a baby, before going back into the kitchen and returning with sweets to feed him.

Maharshi had started crying uncontrollably the moment he walked into her hospital room.

What he saw before him was an old and emaciated shadow of his lively grandmother. She was barely audible. She was bedridden and had two enormous colostomy bags on her stomach. Any food that she ate would leak out through the holes and into the bags. Maharshi was still haunted by her gut-wrenching screams of pain every six hours when the bags were taken out and replaced. She couldn't eat solid food or drink more than a spoonful of water, staying continually parched with thirst.

Maharshi held back tears every time he took his grandmother for her daily walks around the hospital. He had to lift the IV bags for her as she walked; she was too weak to hold them herself.

He had stayed with her for four weeks until he had to return to America to continue college. Before Maharshi left, the doctor had advised the family that another surgery and stitches would solve the problem. Maharshi remembered that conversation quite well. The doctor had laid a reassuring hand on his shoulder and in a fatherly tone said, 'Don't worry at all about your grandma, Son. She'll be up and about the next time you see her, and you'll have to try hard to catch up with her!'

Maharshi had believed the doctor. He had yet to learn how easily lying came to practised tongues.

He had left India fully expecting to see Jyoti Ba when he was due to return six months later. But she seemed to know that she was seeing her grandson for the last time. On the day Maharshi was due to fly back to the US, she had called his father. 'Listen Kashyap, I will not be here when you return. Maharshi is very tender. Please look after him and make sure that he can handle life well.'

The family had attributed this to paranoia and had good reason to believe she'd be fine in a few months.

Sitting in his dorm with his father, Maharshi shook his head. His grandmother had to be fine. The doctor had said it was all taken care of and that she'd be completely healed.

'There's a mistake, Dad. It can't be.'

Kashyap just shook his head sadly in response, and told him what had happened after they had left India.

The doctor who had promised to fix Jyoti Ba's intestines had turned out to be a fraud. He had taken advantage of the family's vulnerability and naivety. By telling everyone what they wanted to hear, he had managed to even deceive Kashyap. He had only intended to keep Jyoti Ba in hospital for as long as possible so that he could profit off the absurdly high expenses of her hospitalization. The family found this out when he bragged about it to a co-worker, who happened to be an old school friend of Kashyap. They also learned that Jyoti Ba's condition was incurable. She was going to die. After talking to Maharshi's parents and uncles, she had decided she'd rather spend her remaining days at home surrounded by her family. She passed away in the arms of her beloved daughter and Maharshi's mother Alpa.

Jyoti Ba's final words were to Maharshi's uncle. 'Tushar, please make sure all my jewellery goes to Maharshi's wife when he marries.'

They had never told Maharshi about these developments.

Maharshi was in shock. He simply sat, dumbfounded, as his father carefully explained everything. Then slowly reality hit him, and the tears came.. But he regained his composure soon enough. Life was strange – in exchange for nineteen years of his grandmother's unconditional love for him, Maharshi had only fifteen minutes of grief to spare for her.

He began wondering how his family would handle the loss. Jitu Dada, his maternal grandfather, was one of the most tender and loving people Maharshi knew. Even when everyone believed that Jyoti Ba was going to be cured, Jitu Dada would only sleep three or four hours each night, waking up out of anxiety at 2 or 3 a.m.. It was understandable: his own father had died of cancer immediately after Jitu Dada finished college, which had left him with the burden of caring for a younger brother, a wife and three children. Maharshi could only imagine the state his poor grandfather must be in now. His grandparents had been married for forty-seven years. In comparison, Maharshi's longest relationship had lasted all of three weeks. The amount of love that would be needed to sustain a marriage for so long was unfathomable to him. He expressed his concern in a voice choked with tears.

'Don't worry Beta, your mom is still there with Dada,' Kashyap consoled his son. 'As are both your uncles. Jitu Dada will be all right.'

Maharshi was relieved, but not much.

Then, something else happened . . . .

Maharshi didn't talk to many people for the next few days, but finally made a plan to hang out with one of his closest friends, Aalok Modi, a week later. Aalok was not his mentor, but was like an elder brother for Maharshi. One evening, they decided to get together and plan something fun for later that night. Aalok had a basketball game that would begin at 9.15, and promised to call when he got out. Maharshi went to dinner with a few other friends before getting back to campus around 10. He then went to a friend's room, where they just sat around chatting.

Aalok never called Maharshi. Instead, at 10.30, Maharshi received a call from someone who was playing in the game. Aalok had collapsed. Before he could even begin to comprehend what that meant, the others in the room received text messages that Aalok had died. Maharshi raced to the hospital just in time to see his friend's body before it was taken to the morgue.

Maharshi hadn't cried in six years until that fateful month of February. Now, he had broken down twice. Aalok's sudden death shook him to the core. He began losing direction in life. In a span of two weeks, he had lost his dear grandmother and one of his best friends. It seemed that misfortune had finally caught up with him, after staying away for the first two decades of his privileged life. Away from home, he had no means to vent his grief. His grades started dropping. His perfect life was slipping from his grasp. It couldn't get any worse. Or so he thought.

In one of its cruel twists, fate had yet another jolt in store for Maharshi. He went home for two weeks, between the end of the spring semester and the start of summer classes. One afternoon he got a call from his father's business partner. He had bad news.

Kashyap had gone out to play tennis early that morning. He felt a sharp pain in his back on the tennis court, and recognized the signs of an imminent heart attack. His partner immediately drove him to a heart specialist for cardiac catheterization. The test showed that he had two active ruptures in a blood vessel known as the Widowmaker Artery, so named for the high fatality rate of patients with that type of lesion. The fact that Kashyap came home alive was miraculous, but his condition was still frail.

Reluctantly, Maharshi went back to Duke after two weeks to start his summer organic chemistry class. Just seven days later, he received a call from his mother – his father had been in a horrific car accident; he had escaped life-threatening injuries by less than a hair's breadth. The new Lexus was completely destroyed.

Maharshi couldn't take it any more. He started losing focus and, along with it, his sense of discretion and the ability to differentiate between right and wrong. He began exercising errors of judgement to the point where he totally destroyed his academic career and morality. His life was falling apart, and Maharshi kept going down a perilous path.

Some people deal with suffering by going into a shell; others become embittered and melancholy. Maharshi became extravagant. He thought that by indulging himself in the best of what life had to offer, he could stave off the grief and stress that continually gnawed at his mind. And yet, with each new passing pleasure, he sank deeper into the ditch he was digging.

Even though his grades got worse, Maharshi was convinced that all would be well; he could always do better in the next exam, write a better paper the next time. But that time never came. He started lying to his parents, making them believe that he was still as brilliant as before; and, to an extent, he was deceiving himself. His behaviour became bad, and he was summoned in front of the university's judicial board. But despite all these blatant signs that he was on the wrong path, Maharshi disregarded everything. All he cared about was short-term pleasure and self-satisfaction that allowed him to hide his sorrow.

A well-wishing friend of Maharshi once tried to halt his spiral downwards. He asked Maharshi what he planned to do after he had completely screwed his life around.

Maharshi scoffed. 'See, the thing about people with trust funds is that, frankly, we don't have to do anything at all. I can afford to live like this my entire life and my only problem would be actually spending all this money!'

His friend was appalled. This wasn't the same guy he had met two and a half years ago at the orientation; this was an unabashedly spoiled brat he could barely recognize any more.

Maharshi's hedonistic lifestyle continued for quite a while before totally collapsing one day. He never thought his parents would find out that he had lost all initiative to do anything productive with his life outside of partying. But they did learn about his many problems and transgressions. Amid his father's shouts of anger and his mother's tears of sorrow, Maharshi kept a stoic face. However, during this altercation, he realized that the game was up. All his self-deception came crashing down, and it dawned upon him how much harm he had caused to his own future. He couldn't bear it. He decided that he was done with the world. He couldn't continue living with the knowledge that all his hopes and dreams, and the hopes and dreams others had for him, were destroyed.

Failure.

Worthless.

Disappointment.

The words cycled through Maharshi's mind again and again and again.

This was it. His darkest hour.

Everything around him blurred. He could see his father yelling and that words were still coming out of his mouth, but he was in a daze in which nothing his father said seemed to matter any more. All that mattered was the cyclone of failure, disappointment, and being worthless. The gold plating had faded from Maharshi's gilded life. All that was left now was the ugly black lead.

His parent's words blended into the background of the room and, for all that he could realize, they were no more distinguishable than the steady hum of the air conditioner.

The path was suddenly exceedingly clear and simple for Maharshi. As he began to walk down it, he felt a supreme detachment from the world around him. How could he not have seen it before? The first step down the road was an excuse. 'I need some water.' Was that actually him speaking?

His father assented, but Maharshi barely noticed. He calmly walked into the kitchen. As he poured the water, he reached into his pocket and began fingering the keys of the Benz. A roadblock suddenly appeared in his plan: how would he get the garage open without the alarm going off and alerting his parents? The solution came to him immediately.

'There's no ice. I'm getting some from the garage.'

Maharshi punched in the digits to deactivate the alarm, and heard the reassuring beep of the alarm turning off.

He still hadn't lost his nerve or the belief that what he was doing was right. If he would be like this the rest of the way, it wouldn't be so bad at all.

Maharshi closed the door behind him. The beep of the car

unlocking was similar to the alarm shutdown. He chuckled as he realized that perhaps approaching the end was making him more aware of things he usually ignored. Since he usually ignored everything that didn't give him instant pleasure, he thought that it was a fitting end.

At least he'd die a tad more aware.

He turned on the car and opened the garage. The plan's completion was suddenly crystal-clear to him as indecision's head reared itself. What would he do? Perhaps he would drive to a new state, abandon the vehicle, and start a new life in poverty and obscurity? Or perhaps he would conveniently wait for a tractor trailer going the other way.

Interstate 485 was just half a mile away. Tractor trailers were always driving by all day and night. He could find one of suitable size very soon. The divider was non-existent at many points. He considered the car. The flagship sedan was built for safety: people who spent $100,000 on a car usually wanted to make sure they didn't die while driving it. For the first time he wished his father still had the old 1988 Corolla lying around. It would have made his life, and its passing, much easier.

Maharshi shook himself out of the doubts. He would decide along the way. No car speeding at 120 miles per hour could save the driver from a head-on collision with an eighteen-wheeler. Not even his prized Mercedes, especially if he was not wearing his seat belt.

He turned his head around and reversed out, into the driveway. As soon as the car was aligned straight, he was prepared to push the accelerator that would inevitably take him away from the house for the last time.

Maharshi didn't get very far.

His mother had already sensed that something was dreadfully wrong with him. She had noticed him withdrawing from the conversation, and could clearly see that he was far from himself. She had kept a watchful eye on him and was waiting in the kitchen when she heard the sound of the car engine turning on.

She ran after him and jumped in front of the car, squarely planting herself in front of it with her hands spread across the hood. Had she been five seconds late, Maharshi's story may have ended here.

Kashyap ran out as well and, possessed with the strength of panic, the couple hauled their son out of the car and into the house.

2

. . . Is Just Before Dawn

'I am beginning to see that all my troubles have their root in a habitual and absolute dependence upon my personal prestige, security, and romantic attachment. When these things go wrong, there is depression . . . We are making demands on circumstances and people that are bound to fail us. The only safe and sure channel of absolute dependence is upon God himself.'
– Bill Wilson

Maharshi couldn't bear to think of the shocked and anguished looks on his parents' faces after he was dragged back into the house. As if on cue, his cell phone vibrated again. Another text message; this time from a different friend. 'Golf at 5?'

Maharshi chuckled. The triviality of the interruptions was amusing, but they were welcome nonetheless. The flashbacks ceased and his pensive mood ended. With his heart still pounding, he walked indoors. His parents were going to arrive soon, and they were going with him to meet his dean.

Kashyap was devastated when he had found out about Maharshi's downfall. He had made it his life's goal for his son to avoid struggles as much as possible, and wanted to pave a smooth road for his future. Now, it appeared as if Maharshi had no future. All of his high spirits and unbounded energy failed him. His own journey had been long and arduous. With his wife and son in tow, his search for success had taken him all over the world. He had worked long hours and ceaselessly put in extra work so that he could provide for his family. He had thought that with Maharshi settled in his studies, he could finally take a break from work and slowly move towards retirement. Those plans had gone down the drain along with Maharshi's life.

Maharshi's mother continually worried about him now. What hurt her the most was Maharshi's total disregard for his own life. The image of his face behind the steering wheel haunted her dreams, and she couldn't sleep for weeks on end. She had always allowed her husband to direct Maharshi's future, while she took care to ensure his well-being along the way. That her son wanted to throw that all away shook her to the core and made her think that she had failed in her role as a mother. All she ever wanted was for Maharshi to be happy, but he clearly wasn't.

Stephen Bryan, Maharshi's dean, cut short his long weekend upon receiving an email from Kashyap, urgently describing the events of the night before. He came to Charlotte personally to speak to Maharshi.

Maharshi's conversation with the dean jolted him as if he had been struck by lightning. He saw exactly how far down his actions had taken him. Confused, guilty of sins of both commission and omission, he desperately wanted help to guide him between right and wrong, between duty and obligation.

What followed was intensive counselling by his parents, their friends and therapists. He slowly came back to his senses. They all had one goal: to make Maharshi realize that happiness did not come from material wealth. If it had, they reasoned, then he would never have been in these dire straits.

Therapy was pointless. The psychiatrist asked what had made him take the final step.

'Well Doc,' Maharshi responded, 'let's start at the beginning. Until about oh, seven years back, I had no permanent home. I was born in India, raised in England, and became a teenager in the United States. Wherever I made friends, I'd have to leave them behind when the time came for us to move again.'

He took a sip of water and continued, 'We finally settled down in Charlotte. After moving and spending all of our savings on a home, we discovered unresolvable philosophical differences among partners, at which point they had to split. At that time there was a fifty-fifty chance that my father would lose his job and we'd be left with almost no money. Well, he didn't lose his job and we became rich – very rich.

'For the next few years, I start living a life most people dream about living. And then, in rapid succession, my grandma dies one of the most painful deaths possible, one of my best friends suddenly dies at the age of 21, and my father almost dies twice in one month. I start losing focus and become depressed, not caring about grades or friends any more, but obviously I can't express this to anyone. Instead, I decide to just go on living the grand life and ignore any damage I was doing to myself. I do this for some time with no one knowing what I'm up to – not my friends, not my parents, no one. So most people now see me as nothing more than a spoiled prick who thinks he's better than anyone else and can behave however he wants because he has rich parents.'

Maharshi paused for a second and drew in a deep breath. 'That is, until one day my parents accidently find out that everything I've told them about my grades, my ambitions – everything – has been a lie. At that point my father calls his attorney and writes me out of his will. Says that he doesn't want a son who does nothing in life but live off his dad's money. Tells me that I should apply for a job at Wal-Mart the next morning, because that's all I'd amount to in life anyway and that I might as well get used to it now. Forget Duke, he says, I already lost that chance. Mom, of course, is basically in shock. Says that she doesn't even know her own son. Wonderful right, Doc?'

'By then, of course, I start believing that I'm worthless. That I've been living a lie for quite a while now. What have I done in the past few years but spend my parents' money? Nothing, right? And that was when it became quite obvious what I had to do.'

'So, tell me Doc, have you ever had a patient who couldn't call a place home until he was thirteen, then was scared of having an unemployed father until fifteen, then lived like a king until nineteen, then lost his grandma and his best friend and almost lost his dad twice, lost interest in his future and did nothing but indulge in whatever money could buy, and finally faced being disowned by his own parents and having everything taken away?'

When the psychiatrist didn't answer, Maharshi gave a dry laugh.

No psychiatrist or psychologist would ever understand who he was and what he needed unless they had lived through the changes he had experienced. His old elitism arose again as he scoffed thinking that a therapist would never be able to afford a lifestyle like his, and never understand what happened when it fell apart.

When Maharshi hit rock bottom emotionally, his family's Indian friends – Deepak Uncle, Bina Aunty, Jagruti Aunty and Gor Uncle in particular – supported him with immeasurable love, compassion, guidance and wisdom. He realized that all these were inbred values within Indian society. This explained why even its poorest and most underprivileged members were still at peace and contented, why Indian slums never had the appalling violence of New York ghettos. Although his pain was compounded by the fact that on his last two trips to India he had witnessed damage caused by terrorists, he also recalled a happiness and resilience that he hadn't seen elsewhere.

It was then that Maharshi started looking back towards India for solace. All popular works on India portrayed it as a backward country, with an uneducated, bigoted populace and rigid system of social exclusion. But that was far from reality. He wanted to experience the India that offered hope and a future to the common man who lived only to be content and without a desire to leave behind any mark; the common man who valued truth, simplicity and morality above material wealth. He wanted to speak to those who had lived in slums, those who had been orphaned, those who were surrounded by despair and yet found peace, and rose from their own ashes like a phoenix.

Maharshi instinctively knew that he would find the answer to his problems in the country of his roots. He knew that he was no Gandhi or Martin Luther King, and that he could never be, so he didn't bother to model himself on them. Nor did he want to follow the path of celebrities and other well-known people; he had seen enough of society to know that skeletons hid in the closets of all figureheads of success. He wanted to experience the life millions of ordinary Indians had, with the ability to sleep contentedly each night and the ability to die peacefully. He wanted to learn how to live fully, how to not be deterred by any adversity.

Maharshi knew only one person who had these traits. That person's words were not based on bookish knowledge, but on his own sufferings and struggles. It was Bhogi, his paternal grandfather, who was born in a small village in a little mud-brick hut and had lost both his parents before reaching his teens. He was a man who had faced the wrath of droughts, locust swarms and starvation, and yet managed to climb up to the highest position in his field. In spite of his non-judgemental nature, he had been pulled into family feuds and disputes that eventually led to the death of an unborn child, and the alcoholism and suicide of his oldest son. His was a life story full of struggle, death and destruction. He rose only to fall, then rose again and then fell down again.

It fell on Bhogi to bury three generations of his family; yet he saw optimism everywhere and injustice nowhere. He looked at both adverse and favourable incidents through the solemn lens of karma and destiny, and always sought an opportunity to serve humanity and sow the seeds of hope.

It was to him that Maharshi now turned. He called Bhogi the next morning. He asked his grandfather about Jyoti Ba and Aalok's deaths, about why people died prematurely when life had just begun for them.

Bhogi replied, 'We all are like raindrops, Son, heading towards the ocean that is God. Raindrops slowly collect to form streams. Streams then form rivers, which finally reach the eternal ocean. Like streams, we form families, societies and nations; all that eventually blends in with the ocean. But some raindrops fall on plain soil and never make it to the ocean. It may seem that those raindrops have fallen in vain. But they instead quench the thirst of plants, animals, and people. If it wasn't for those raindrops, life wouldn't exist. Similarly, though it may seem to you that life was snatched from people without allowing their lives to bear fruit, the truth is that their lives too had an impact on this earth during their limited time here. No life is ever in vain.'

His words were so convincing and soothing that Maharshi asked, 'Bhogi Dada! Where did you learn this? Which scriptures taught you this?'

'There is no better book than the book of life,' Bhogi explained. 'Every chapter in the book of life has plenty of lessons to offer. There are no tragedies, just metamorphoses. I have cried so many times in my early life that when my son – your uncle – killed himself, I almost had no tears left and yet I did not lose my faith. You see, those who ignore life and try to learn from books and scriptures never really learn anything, and will have to be reborn.'

'Will you share your life's book with me, Dada?'

'Only if you promise to learn from it, Son.'

Maharshi decided it was time to go to India. He left three days later.

3

The Quest for Happiness

'The essence of optimism is that it takes no account of the present, but it is a source of inspiration, of vitality and hope where others have resigned; it enables a man to hold his head high, to claim the future for himself and not to abandon it to his enemy.' – Dietrich Bonhoeffer

Uneasy dreams haunted Maharshi as he fell asleep on the flight to Ahmedabad. Driving along roads thronged by the poor made him feel no better. He was now torn between the luxuries that his elitist lifestyle afforded him and the thought that millions of Indians lived below the poverty line, not knowing where the next meal would come from. Maharshi began to ponder over what he had done to deserve such amenities and felt all the more guilty that he had wanted to throw them all away. He saw life's unfairness in full flow and wondered why only a privileged few born in Western societies had been blessed with a multitude of resources. While children born in Third World countries had to battle hunger, poverty, violence, death and destruction almost on a daily basis, well-heeled kids watched television or played computer games. Having studied in Europe and the USA, Maharshi had been taught to ask questions when he felt he didn't understand something and he also had a detailed concept of human rights and suffering. But who could he go to in order to learn what would happen to the millions of poor souls? Was there someone who could reassure him about life's true meaning and its implications?

Everything seemed to be colluding at once to bring him down. Maharshi was sick to the stomach that he had wasted his life so far in the pursuit of transient pleasures. He recalled with shame and disgust how he used to scoff when the food he was served wasn't exactly to his taste. He found it horrible that while the overwhelming majority of the poor in Mumbai wore what they could scrape by with, he had thought that any shirt under $40 was unworthy of touching his skin.

The amount of poverty that Maharshi observed was at once eye-opening and shocking. The streets were lined with malnourished, anonymous Indians who would spend their entire lives beneath the radar of government services and the notice of everyone else. Their lives were thwarted by the walls of socio-economic barriers and despite being only about 5 feet away from the rest of society, they could well have been separated by thousands of miles.

Maharshi began to wonder if anyone could really rise up from the wretched condition of the average Indian slum dweller. The only success stories that emerged out of those dark depths always involved organized crime and violence and usually resulted in a lavish lifestyle for a few years before being arrested or gunned down by the age of forty. The occasional legitimate success story would come up, à la *Slumdog Millionaire*, but Maharshi wondered just how common such inspiring accounts really were – maybe one in a million. He wanted to know if it was actually possible for an individual to escape the anonymous ranks of the starving at the street corners and become a success, or whether that class of Indians was doomed to destitution for ever. The many difficulties faced in overcoming such a situation made it seem utterly impossible to someone as pampered as him. The inability to obtain a proper education as a result of having spent an entire life trying to make ends meet, coupled with the lack of education among parents, seemed to make the perfect story of inescapability, rendering the unfortunate doomed to spend their entire lives in the same filthy shantytowns like their fathers and forefathers. Menial labour jobs for a mere pittance would be their fate.

However, this seemed far too bleak to be true. There ought to have been stories of people who had escaped the misery of living below the poverty line in India. Maharshi refused to believe that the gap between the two realms was unbridgeable.

He was actually seeking solace and comfort for himself. He was looking for hope and stories of success, not of world-renowned celebrities, but of those who had been through difficult times through poverty and suffering and yet never lost their hope for a bright future. He wanted to meet someone who could inspire him and millions like him; who was not aspiring for titles or recognition, but for peace, simplicity and happiness. He was striving to meet someone who sought an opportunity to help and serve the helpless despite his own tragedies; someone who brought light to others even if it meant burning his own hands in the process.

Slowly a face started emerging before his mind's eye, a face with many wrinkles that reflected the countless deaths it had encountered and the untold pains it had suffered, with burn marks from injuries sustained while trying to play the role of the breadwinner in the family. That face became brighter and brighter, with scattered white hair over the shiny head, perhaps indicating the man's age and wisdom. His face bore a pensive look, but still shone with happiness and inner brightness. In spite of the pain of having performed the last rites of three generations, he still had faith in life and destiny.

The face belonged to none other than Bhogi, Maharshi's grandfather.

Maharshi was aware that his own grandfather had been one of the unfortunate millions in India. He had experienced death, poverty, devastation and slavery throughout his life. He had seen some of his family members die in succession in the prime of their lives, while others had been victims of hate. And his eldest son had ended his own life.

Bhogi had lived through ruthless killing and slaughtering on a scale that Maharshi would hopefully never witness. He had seen the massacre of millions in the name of religion, starting from the 1947 India-Pakistan Partition riots – riots that had engulfed India in a wildfire of funeral pyres, looting and plundering. He had also suffered severe famines, when people in the remote areas of India had, quite literally, nothing to eat except cacti and, if they were lucky, some grains found embedded in animal excreta. His quiet face hid a lifetime filled with struggles of different kinds and decades of hardship and loss. It was to him that Maharshi finally opened up fully.

Maharshi spent the next few weeks listening to his grandfather's story; his journey through countless tragedies. They sat on a khaatlo, Bhogi's makeshift bed, made out of lead pipes assembled together with cotton ropes tied in a criss-cross fashion that provided a base for a thin mattress at night. Despite the significant wealth he had accumulated, Bhogi had been sleeping in the same bed for the past thirty years. His living space was a terrace measuring 10x15 feet. He woke up at 7 each morning and slept at 10 every night. His routine was so meticulously fixed that one could easily set their clock by it. Maharshi was somewhat amused as to how different their ideas about necessities were. His bed and sheets alone probably cost more than all of his grandfather's possessions. There had often been nights when Maharshi stayed up partying until 10 in the morning and then slept till 7 p.m.

Bhogi's face was dark and tanned – the result of having spent decades roaming under the scorching Indian sun, irrespective of the heat and cold, just so he could meet his basic needs. The many scars and wrinkles on his face reflected neglect and the lack of basic healthcare in his childhood. He had a hole in his left ear lobe from a past skin infection. But still, his face was always bright; his voice low, firm and soothing. It occurred to Maharshi that he had never heard his grandfather raise his voice at anyone.

Maharshi was looking for something beyond those weather-beaten features. Bhogi's eyes had long dried up from shedding tears all his life. Despite the obvious marks of deep-seated wounds on his visage that he never complained about, Bhogi had an almost tranquil aura that gave Maharshi a feeling of comfort just by sitting with his grandfather.

Maharshi said to him, 'Dada, I'm very disturbed at the pain

and suffering of people around the world. I'm just as uncertain about myself. I live a life based on lies and deceits every day. The only reason to study is so that I can afford more material things. Every day I turn on a news channel and see reports of violence, suicide bombings, war and starvation. I feel quite gloomy about the future of my generation and, indeed, my own future. I'm afraid that I see very little hope. Can you share experiences from your life? What it was that made you so resilient to the shivers and quakes that fate sends our way?'

'Maharshi Beta, I have lived many decades of life and died several times in my own lifetime as well. Let me tell you that there is always hope. There is no pain or suffering. Everyone is born with the destiny that will determine their life. Everyone is a creation of the Lord and we all are children of God. He will never give us any trouble that we cannot handle.'

'But Dada,' Maharshi interrupted, 'you know pretty much what I have been through at such a tender age. When all my friends were enjoying their lives with their girlfriends, I was finding reasons to hide and cry and grieve for the untimely and cruel death of Jyoti Ba. Just around the time when I recovered, I had to sit by the body of one of my best friends. Above all, you know, Father had a heart attack. How then can you say that life is fair and God is always with us?'

Maharshi felt that Bhogi was somewhat apathetic to his personal issues as they had a distance of two generations and 10,000 miles between them.

'No my dear boy, don't say that,' Bhogi responded. 'God always loves His creations. You cannot look at life in the context of just one point in time. The biggest problem you have is that from your birth onwards, you have always looked at life through the eyes of a lion. Just like the lion, you have been raised to look at life as if it is your prey. You want to be successful, see life as a game that is to be won. But even if you do win, you would merely eat the prey and then want more. Your happiness at having won and eaten would be transitory at best. There is a big difference between being successful and being happy; something I'm sure you've already figured out, else you wouldn't be here asking me these questions right now. If you really want to enjoy the Almighty's glory, you have to look at life in all its totality. Look at life from the view of the eagle that soars through the air, thousands of feet above the ground.'

He continued, 'A lion is powerful, there is no doubt about that, but his vision is always fixated on his prey – everywhere he looks, he does so with the vision of a predator waiting to pounce. The lion misses out on the beauty that is around him. When he sees a lake, he focuses on the gazelles drinking from it. He misses the beauty that is the lake itself, and its surrounding trees buzzing with life. The lion is built this way by nature; if it focused on natural beauty, it wouldn't have food to eat. But man is different. When you look at life from the height and perspective of a distant observer, like the bird that soars far above the earth, then, and only then, will you will be able to see Mother Nature in its original form; and only from that perspective will you be able to see life's real intricacies, and all your questions will be answered.'

'I heard a story from someone almost a year ago that will answer your queries perfectly. It was a conversation between an apathetic professor and his student. The professor said that if God created everything he must have created evil, since it existed, and that God was therefore evil. He challenged his students to prove him wrong. One of his students was none other than Einstein. He responded by asking, "Sir, does cold exist?" The professor replied, "Of course it exists." Einstein said, "No Sir, it does not. There is no energy that creates cold. Cold is simply an absence of the energy of heat. There is no such thing as cold energy." He then asked, "Sir, does darkness exist?" The professor, less surely this time, said, "Yes, it does." Einstein then countered, "No Sir, darkness does not exist. Darkness is the absence of light. Light can be studied but darkness cannot." Finally, Einstein asked if evil existed. More confidently, the professor said that it did, judging by the violence and malice present in the world. Einstein stated, "No Sir, evil doesn't exist. Like cold and darkness, evil and unhappiness are simply the absence of God's presence in the hearts and minds of wrongdoers."'

Maharshi wryly remarked that the story Bhogi had heard sounded more like an urban legend than fact.

Bhogi responded, 'So what if the story isn't true, or if Einstein didn't actually say all that? Does that make the logic that it expresses any less sound or convincing? Once again Beta, you are too engrossed in the details for you to see the big picture or grasp its meaning.'

Maharshi didn't say anything.

Bhogi then added, 'The biggest problem that you have, Beta, is your approach to life. You have always lived life with a goal in mind. You want to become rich, you want to be successful. Everything is just a means to that end. You start at point A, which is where you were when you went to college, and all you can see beyond that is point Z, where you're living a life of ease and luxury. You miss out on B through Y. It isn't your fault; society has raised you to look at life like this. It is the journey from B through Y, however, that will teach you to embrace the happiness that life has to offer. And by the time you complete that journey, you will find that the material goods you looked for at point Z have lost their importance.'

Finally, Bhogi gently said, 'You know how my life began, and you can see me now. But let me tell you the story of my B through Y.'

And so he began, with his birth in 1934.

4

The Beginning

'Birth and death are not two different states, but they are different aspects of the same state. There is as little reason to deplore the one as there is to be pleased over the other.' – Mahatma Gandhi

The India of the 1930s, as remembered by the world today, was an enchanting fairy tale. It speaks of an age when the Union Jack arrogantly flew atop the Red Fort. It is reminiscent of the maharajas' manicured cricket grounds and the leisurely polo clubs of the British sahibs. It regales us with pictures of the cavernous mansions of nawabs and the debauchery that occurred within. It was a time when the sun had not set on the British empire, and India was a jewel in its crown.

Bhogi's birth took place in an era of lavish cantonments of British armies, maintaining law and order across vast lands, and when the Queen of England was still called the Empress of India. Those were the years of rich estates of the royalty, contrasting with the arid land, scanty crops and backbreaking labour of the masses. Those were the years of two separate Indias. One was the romanticized country of the rich and powerful aristocracy, and then there was the country of millions of poor villagers struggling to make ends meet every single day. Those were the years when, to find the true India, one would journey not to the darbars of rajas or the palaces of the civil service agents, but to the mud and straw huts of the many isolated villages scattered across the dusty Deccan Plateau.

This India was also remembered for something else. While the all-powerful bureaucrats of the Indian Civil Service spent their days sipping gin on their sprawling verandas and their nights at sumptuous feasts and balls, one emaciated man spent his days walking and his nights sleeping in peasants' huts. His destination was the sea and his goal was to defy the empire. With nothing more than a bamboo stick in his hand and hard leather sandals on his blistered feet the 'half naked fakir', as Churchill referred to him, now stood at the head of the masses of India, calling for freedom.

Mohandas Karamchand Gandhi, throughout his journey from a nervous barrister to Mahatma and the idol of millions, always insisted that he himself never had any power. Rather, he asserted, the power was held by the many millions of poor villagers who made up the bulk of India. The power to overthrow the British wasn't in the cities and with the educated elite who lived in them, but in the many small remote villages full of starving peasants. They, he said, were the real India. And the story of Maharshi's grandfather begins in one of those villages called Detroj.

Situated about 50km from the desert, Detroj comprised around a thousand villagers residing in over half a square km of land. Living in close proximity to one another had made them not just neighbours, but they had grown to become close friends.

Bhogi was born on 9 January 1934 to Mohanlal and Kashi Patel. The unusually bitter chill of the winter, coupled with rumours of armed dacoit gangs taking up residence in the hills nearby, had caused the entire village to go to sleep even earlier than usual, with the doors barred and windows bolted. Mohanlal's sleep was quickly interrupted with a scream from his nine-month pregnant wife who felt her first contractions. Trying to keep Kashi calm while he struggled to put on a dhoti, Mohanlal made for an amusing sight. He woke up Kashi's sister, who was there to serve as a midwife. As she attended to Kashi, Mohanlal woke up the many family members who were staying with them.

Soon, the lanterns began to blaze as the entire extended family gathered around. The women wrapped themselves in handmade cloth shawls, while the men exchanged cheery grins as all huddled for warmth against the biting cold. And yet, they sat without complaining, eagerly awaiting the most significant event in a parent's life: the arrival of a baby. Bhikhu, Mohanlal's and Kashi's year-old toddler who had been endlessly applauded for the past week for his crowning achievement of learning to walk, sat crossly due to the lack of attention. Mohanlal himself had been born a month premature and had miraculously survived under the tender care of his mother, but had remained frail and physically weak since birth. All he could do at the moment was pace around his tiny mud-brick home, fervently praying that his child would not have to suffer as he had. The words that had been spoken to him the night before rang through his head.

Armed with a jug full of holy water and a bowl of red vermilion, a priest had paid a visit to the couple the previous night. While chanting a sequence of Sanskrit mantras, which, in all likelihood he didn't fully understand himself, he sprayed the mother and her belly with the holy water and applied the vermilion to her forehead, ensuring that the evil eye would stay away and that the child's birth into the world would go well. To signify the conclusion of the ceremony, a coconut was smashed on the ground. After feeling the kicks of the baby from within the womb, the priest exchanged a few words with Mohanlal.

Mohanlal immediately paid the priest the sum he requested. 'Please tell me that I'll have a male heir,' Mohanlal begged.

Satisfied with the amount he had been paid, the priest gave a positive response. 'I have looked at the sky. The alignment of Mars and Jupiter is a favourable one. By the grace of the gods residing above, I am very sure that by the end of the week a baby boy will be born to you and your wife.'

In that era, the occult was taken very seriously. Of more consequence than what was before one's eyes was what the heavens spelt and, conveniently enough, the priests forbade anyone outside their ranks from interpreting them.

The priest's prediction replayed over and over again in Mohanlal's mind. He was a poor man. Due to his physical weakness, he had never been able to become a capable farmer, and he was able to only grow enough to provide for his wife and elderly mother. He already had a son to take care of. His brother had just passed away, leaving Mohanlal responsible for looking after his brother's wife and her two young sons. To have another boy in the family would be a blessing, a second heir to carry on his name – in case the first died – and an extra hand when it came to ploughing the fields. More importantly, a son did not bring the burden of having to pay dowry when it came to marriage.

All these thoughts of finances and boys and marriage quickly faded from Mohanlal's mind though, when he heard Kashi's ear-splitting scream as her contractions suddenly became stronger.

The women around immediately began reassuring her. Each had her own piece of advice and experience.

'Don't worry; it won't take more than a few minutes.'

'Push harder. Don't think, and just push.'

'My Vimla took five hours; this is nothing in comparison.'

None of these eager comments really registered in Kashi's mind. As the baby slowly emerged, Kashi's shrieks were the only sound that punctuated the silence of the house. The women were gathered together and, under the direction of the barber who doubled as a temporary surgeon, urged her to push harder and offered to hold her hands which were often violently crushed when another contraction ripped through Kashi's body.

Finally, after two gruelling hours of labour and with the help of Kashi's sister, Bhogi Mohanlal Patel came out of his mother's womb. With a rusted pair of scissors, the barber cut the umbilical cord. He then wrapped up the placenta in a white cloth to be left in the jungle for animals to feed on.

Following the Patidar tradition, immediately after the birth, Kashi took Bhogi to her parents' home in Dangarva. Traditionally, the birth was to have taken place there, but her mother had fallen ill and it was feared that her sickness would be passed on to Kashi. After the birth, however, Kashi lived at her parents' house for the next six months. There she was able to relax and recuperate from the ordeal that was childbirth in a tiny mud-brick house under the care of a barber. Her mother, who had recovered by then, constantly fussed over Kashi, giving her extra vegetables, which meant that the rest of the family would have to occasionally forgo their share. Any extra ghee was spared for Kashi as she had to nurse Bhogi several times a day.

Those six months were bliss for Kashi and Bhogi. With the innocence that newborns possess, Bhogi found joy and satisfaction in the simplest things, be it a smile on his grandfather's face or pulling his grandmother's hair. Kashi was equally happy, not having to cook, clean or suffer from any of the daily toils of the average Indian housewife.

Unfortunately, all good things come to an end, as did Kashi's comfortable stay at her parents' home. She finally returned, with some trepidation, to her husband's house to resume the duties of a wife in her household. When she arrived, she had a candid discussion with her husband. 'Mohanlal, thank God that you are here to take care of this family. After her husband's death, Santok can barely manage to scrape by from day to day.'

Mohanlal gave a grim look of acknowledgement as he said, 'I know. Without a man to till the fields, there simply is no way for a family to live. I can't imagine what she'd do without me. In fact, I can't imagine what would happen to our family if something were to ever happen to me.'

Alarmed, Kashi admonished him. 'Oh, don't even begin to say such things! How could we possibly raise a family without a father?'

Mohanlal laughed in response and said, 'Oh, don't make such a fuss. I'm here, am I not? And I'm not suddenly going to drop dead one day.'

Over the next few years, as Bhogi grew up, life became a dull routine. Mohanlal, Kashi and Santok rose from their khaatlos every morning at the crack of dawn. Their daily cycle kept up with the cycle of the sun, as there were no lights or electricity. A kerosene lamp with a cotton wick was a necessity and a candle was a piece of luxury reserved for the rich and privileged zamindars.

They walked outside and broke a piece of twig into daatan to clean their teeth – toothpastes and brushes were a staple of the urban elite and their existence was unknown in the village. And yet, this never detracted from good dental health. Each of them placed a daatan in their mouths and chewed on it. As the wood became wet and was crushed bristles appeared and rubbed against the teeth, effectively scrubbing them clean. Along with the daatan they also tried to carry out their morning ablutions in a secluded place within walking distance.

When Bhogi was still young, Kashi started her day by tenderly breast-feeding him, and then walked outside with a bucket. There the family's most prized possessions, two strong black gaurs, were tethered. She gently milked both the buffaloes and collected the fresh, sweet milk into the bucket. Santok waited inside with a wooden rod and a small pot. Kashi poured half the milk into the pot and the remaining into six small earthen cups for each member of the family to drink as their breakfast.

While Kashi busied herself with preparing lunch, Santok's son Mangal, who studied in the village school, led the buffaloes to a nearby communal animal well from where they drank their fill. He then brought them home and went off again to collect grass for the buffaloes to eat. Mohanlal then left the house with the buffaloes and proceeded to the fields. There he hitched them up to a plough and began farming. He planted everything, from cotton to grains, on his various small plots of land, bringing in enough food for the family to eat and also crops to sell for some additional money.

While Mohanlal worked, Santok used the buffalo milk that Kashi gave her to make a mervan, or a mixture that would end up as ghee. She first curdled the milk, then churned the curdled milk from the day before by hand until butter was formed. She then placed the pot of butter atop their stove –a stone base that was covered with coal and then lit – with a small dish over it. She let the butter heat until the surface became a frothy white. Finally, she emptied the liquid, which was now pure ghee, into a large pot. Then she went around the neighbourhood, selling about half of the ghee to neighbours who didn't have the money to own cattle or to those who had so much money that they chose not to make their own ghee. On her way home Santok made a stop at the drinking well and brought back pots of water, some of them balanced on her head.

At home, Kashi took the vegetables out of their pot-in-pot cooler. While it would not be known to the world for another thirty years or so, this ingenious cooling system was long in use in most villages of India. One small pot was placed within a large pot, with a layer of wet sand in-between the two. Vegetables were then placed inside the small pot. As the heat outside increased, the water in the sand slowly evaporated out of the pores in the outer pot, cooling the one within much in the same way as sweat cools the human body.

Next, Kashi made rotis for lunch. To cook these flat round pieces of bread, Kashi first kneaded dough from the flour of the grains the family grew in their field and then roasted them over a tawa they had purchased from the Jain store. The Jains of the time made their living selling goods and lending money, and each village typically had at least one who served as the town merchant. After labouring in the heat from the cooking fire, coupled with the raging sun outside, Kashi finally prepared a treat – nimbu pani, the Indian version of lemonade made by squeezing the juice from limes into water, adding salt and a dash of sugar.

At noon, the heat outside became unbearable and Mohanlal returned home. Kashi served him with a cool glass of nimbu pani, after which both of them took a well-deserved nap, sleeping through the hottest hours of the day. As the afternoon passed, they woke up and resumed work. When the sun started to set, Mohanlal came back home from the field. Kashi served him dinner; the meal comprising, once again, vegetables and roti.

In this way, the family managed to stay afloat. While they were not affluent by any means, they weren't on the brink of starvation either. Through the efforts of Mohanlal, Kashi, and Santok, Ranchhod and Mangal – Santok's two sons – were spared most of the work others of their age had to do, and they could attend the village school that was up to the seventh grade.

One night, Santok approached Mohanlal and Kashi.

'Mohanlal, Kashi, I wanted to tell you how grateful I am to you for everything you've done for me.'

'Santok, you don't even have to mention it,' Mohanlal said.

'No, really. When my husband died, I was in absolute shock. I had no idea how I would take care of two children. Ranchhod and Mangal would have gone hungry and starved had it not been for you.'

'I really think you're exaggerating our kindness to you.'

'No, no. When my husband died, he left us with almost nothing. We had a buffalo, but no one to tend to it. We had a few acres of land, but no one to till it. We couldn't have possibly lived without your help.'

'It's really all right,' Kashi added. 'We've taken care of Bhogi and Bhikhu, and we can take care of Ranchhod and Mangal too. Everything will be OK.'

Just when it seemed that all was well in the household, tragedy struck.

It came in the form of a stiff neck and a sharp headache for Bhikhu and he was soon compounded with high fever, painful joints and drowsiness. Within hours, Bhikhu's body was covered with red spots all over and he started becoming cold and numb. Immediately the barber-surgeon was called for and when he was unable to explain the symptoms, they asked the child where he had been the past week.

As it turned out, the symptoms began a day after Bhikhu and two friends, on a dare, entered a samshan. The barber contacted the families of Bhikhu's friends and found that both of them also shared similar symptoms. The barber made his prognosis: they had been possessed by malevolent demonic entities, evil spirits that were often said to make a crematorium their abode.

'I am just a man of medicine,' the barber told Kashi, who was deeply worried. 'This is far beyond my ability to fix. There is a spirit, a demonic one, within this child. I must go now; else it may decide to enter my body. Keep him alone until the priest arrives.'

The barber left the house and sent a boy to summon the priest from the nearby temple. The priest arrived as soon as he could, armed with a book of prayers and a bowl of blessed water brought years ago from the Ganges river.

The Brahmin immediately announced that he felt the presence of a demonic entity that had taken up residence inside the boy's body. He instantly started his rite: 'In the name of the blessed Hanuman who defeated the evils of the world, be gone from this place! Be gone and leave alone all whom you now afflict!'

His countenance was grave as he spoke to Santok, who had taken to keeping vigil outside Bhikhu's room, not being brave enough to confront the 'demon' alone.

The priest wasn't particularly reassuring.

'The trials of harbouring such an evil being in one's body are harsh indeed. Only the blessed Hanuman can fight off such a being, and the price will be great,' he asserted.

Santok beseeched, 'Oh, in the name of God, please do all that you can for the poor boy. He is too young to suffer like this!'

The Brahmin began a ritual of exorcism to remove the demon from the boy to cure him. He placed red-hot coals on

Bhikhu's chest, trying to make residence of the ghost in the body unviable. With a roar he chanted 'Jai Bajrang Bali!' and began to beat the boy's chest, trying to eject the devil that supposedly lay within. As the priest burned him, Bhikhu could only cry out in pain.

With another frightening roar, the priest began reciting the *Hanuman Chalisa* out loud – forty verses recounting Hanuman's invocation to defeat demons and evil forces.

The neighbours, shocked by the alternating shouts of the priest and the piteous screams of the burned boy, gathered outside, though none dared to enter, frightened as they were at the idea of demonic possession into their own bodies. After a gruelling hour, the priest announced that the demon had been removed, and left to perform similar exorcisms on the other two children who were afflicted.

Further weakened by the assaults his body had just suffered, Bhikhu passed into a state of unconsciousness and, during the night, into death. The other two boys soon followed his lead, and the screams from the house were replaced by sobs.

It was later found that the priest himself began to exhibit the symptoms that Bhikhu had, but he managed to recover. It seemed now that the prognosis was correct. The ceremony expelling the demon had succeeded, and the demon chose to make the body of the priest his new residence. The trauma of possession was too much for these three-year-old boys to endure, and so they all died. The priest though, with his knowledge of the supernatural, along with age and experience, was able to fight the entity off and therefore recovered.

Of course, what had then been attributed to a demonic possession would in all likelihood today be diagnosed as an infection of bacterial meningitis, one that the three children caught in the cemetery and transmitted to the priest. The fragile and undernourished children, weakened by the painful burns of the exorcism, proved easy prey for the disease while the priest, being older and in the prime of health, was able to fight it off.

Bhogi was too young to understand what had happened. He quietly watched Bhikhu's body being washed and wrapped in white cloth. He curiously saw the priest from a nearby village softly utter phrases that made no sense whatsoever to him. Still only able to speak in partial sentences Bhogi tugged on his parents' white clothes, asking what was happening. His mother's body racked with sobs, and nothing she said made any sense to little Bhogi. His father stood by mutely. Finally, his maternal uncle picked him up and explained to him that his brother had decided to go to heaven and live with the gods a little earlier than most people did, and that his parents were sad that he left so early. Bhogi accepted this as the truth and followed his father and the village men as they placed Bhikhu's body onto a pyre of wood, and watched as the body was lit. As he was watching, he thought he saw something rising to heaven with the smoke. Suddenly, Bhogi started wondering why his brother decided to leave him. Was it because he didn't like playing with him? His innocent mind, trying to grapple with an idea hitherto unknown to him, began to place blame on himself for driving his brother away.

5

The Tempest Gathers

'The odds are six to five that the light in the end of the tunnel is the headlight of an oncoming train '– Paul Dickson

A blanket of silence descended on the humble hut that Bhogi called home. There was that deep stillness typical in a house of mourning, and even the passage of time failed to pierce that gloom. Kashi appeared as if the will to live had deserted her entirely. The fierce love that renders all children so dear to their mothers had turned into grief so profound that a smile rarely lit up her face. All she was left with now was her surviving son, and she refused to let him out of her sight for too long.

Bhogi's father exhibited grief of a different kind. While Kashi frequently burst into tears, Mohanlal became introverted and reticent. He rarely spoke more than a sentence at a time and his voice was perpetually flat, as if someone had snatched all emotion from him and left an empty shell behind. To make matters worse, his health began to deteriorate and the previous ailments that had afflicted him took a turn for the worse.

Bhogi was the worst hit though. He still couldn't comprehend the concept of death and believed that his brother had merely left his home for God's house for some inexplicable reason. He continually racked his mind and tried to think of reasons why his brother had decided to leave him. He finally came to the conclusion that his brother didn't like him. This thought turned into an obsession and Bhogi blamed himself for Bhikhu's death. He became so withdrawn and spoke so little that his parents began to suspect that he was mentally retarded. They weren't the only ones who reached this conclusion; the neighbourhood was rife with rumours of 'Mohanlal's stupid son'. Inevitably, this talk reached the other children of the neighbourhood, who incessantly insulted Bhogi for his supposed inability to speak.

Nevertheless, Bhogi managed to find one constant companion.

As he was walking down the street one day, Bhogi noticed that he was being followed. It wasn't a man or child who was following him, but one of the many neighbourhood stray dogs. This particular one had a large white stripe across its brown head. It seemed to have sensed and shared Bhogi's loneliness. Bhogi remembered that he had never seen this dog with the usual pack of strays and that it always seemed to be wandering by itself. It seemed to be unusually drawn to Bhogi, as if his loneliness played the part of a magnet attracting other lost souls.

'Are you also like me? Does no one else want you? Don't worry; I'll be there for you. Do you have a name?'

The dog merely barked in response.

'I know! I'll call you Kalio!'

And from then onwards, Bhogi adopted Kalio as his own. He fed the dog extra rotis out of his own meals, sometimes even hiding his share and pretending to eat it just so that he could give it to the dog eventually. Mohanlal caught him a few times and slapped him for 'being such a fool that he uses his father's work to feed dogs!' Still, Bhogi didn't stop doing so and occasionally even treated the dog to milk from the buffalo.

One day, as he was walking outside with his trusted companion, Bhogi walked in on a gilli danda game and accidentally ruined the stroke. The kids became very angry.

'Hey retard, where do you think you're going?' one began.

Another followed, 'Yeah, what's the matter, you have no friends apart from that damn dog?'

'Of course he doesn't, or else he'd do something besides moping around all day with him,' a third replied.

The de facto leader of the bunch, Jeevan, was a particularly unpleasant one.

He leered at Bhogi and mercilessly yelled, 'Haha, look at him crying. A weak little girl. Why doesn't that bitch of yours come and protect you?'

Jeevan went so far as to push Bhogi and spit on his face. Bhogi quietly got up and walked away. As he did, his frustration was so great that he even kicked Kalio as he left.

It was dinner time in the Patel household and Bhogi was missing. They called their neighbours for help, and people went to every corner of the village looking for him. As the family returned home, they noticed Kalio barking outside their house. At first they paid no attention to the dog until it came up to the front and incessantly barked. As soon as Mohanlal opened the door, the dog ran up the street, halted and barked again as if to indicate that Mohanlal should follow him. Mohanlal and two other men did and the dog led them all the way out to the samshan. There they saw Bhogi sitting cross-legged on the ground, surrounded by ashes and bones of bodies burned long ago.

Mohanlal seized his son by the neck and dragged him home in a rage. It had not escaped his mind that this was the location where Bhikhu had been 'possessed' by the evil spirit, and the fear of the same happening to Bhogi only added to his fury. On the way home, Mohanlal tore off a stick from a tree and the moment Bhogi entered the house, Mohanlal began to viciously beat him with it. That night Bhogi was given the most severe thrashing of his life. When his father finished, his mother began. Although he furiously shed tears and let out grunts of pain, Bhogi didn't say a word about why he had gone to the saashan and not returned when darkness fell.

Finally when his father, frustrated with his silence, demanded to know why Bhogi had gone there, he quietly began to speak. 'I know why Bhikhu left. It was because of me. I don't think he liked me very much. And then, all the boys were making fun of me and pushing me, and I thought it was because I didn't have a brother to protect me. So I went there to try and talk Bhikhu into coming back, but it didn't work.'

All the rage left Mohanlal and was replaced with a overwhelming remorse. He tenderly embraced Bhogi and for the next hour softly whispered to Bhogi that Bhikhu did not leave because of any member of the family. While biting back hot tears himself, he calmly explained, 'Beta Bhogi, Bhikhu's time had come to depart for heaven at the invitation of the gods residing high up in the sky. No one can refuse the call of the gods to their heavenly abode. We all will finally leave this place and go back to God Almighty.'

Little Bhogi nodded his head as if he understood every word. He was a patient listener. He slowly shared his concerns, 'Bapu, then who else is going to God's house in the sky? Do you know if anyone else has received a call from God?' Bhogi was hiding his own fear of losing his parents or any of his cousins. He knew that Ranchhod's and Mangal's father too had moved up in the skies to God's residence long before Bhogi was even born.

'No one, Son!' Mohanlal emphasized to alleviate Bhogi's worries. 'God will let us all live together for many years, and only when one gets very old and weak and fragile will God take them back to their place.'

Bhogi continued to nod his head. He still had many questions about why then had Bhikhu gone up so soon; he was not old. But Bhogi thought it was best not to ask too many questions.

By then Mohanlal had calmed down. He failed to realize that Bhogi did not have a chance to understand the sudden death of his brother. Finally, he reaffirmed his love for Bhogi and softly wept as he guiltily tended to the raw wounds that Bhogi's tender skin had suffered from the ordeal of the night. Despite his aching body, for the first night in four months,

Bhogi was able to sleep in peace, finally understanding that his brother's death had nothing to do with him.

As the months passed, so did the grief. It was finally overcomed by the joyous news that Kashi had become pregnant for the third time. The carnival that had visited their home four years ago arrived once again, though Mohanlal's health was not in the best shape. Once again, the house was filled with extended family members eagerly helping Kashi with her household duties. Once again, priests made regular visits to their home to bless the unborn child. Kashi had her forehead smeared with vermilion and her face sprayed with holy water yet again.

When the eve of her pregnancy drew nearer, she was taken to her parents' home. After fervent prayers and hours of labour, another son was born to her: Bhailal Mohanlal Patel. Following tradition, Kashi spent the next six months in the haven that was her parents' house. But this time the idyllic getaway was tragically cut short.

It happened on another cold night in the winter of 1938, eerily similar to the night Bhogi had been born. He was beginning to learn and cope with the new arrival in the family, his twenty-day-old younger brother Bhailal. So far Bhogi had been the focus of his parents' attention. Suddenly he had to deal with feelings of jealousy after seeing the entire family coo over the newborn. Bhogi was already having misgivings about Bhailal, and had not seen his father for almost four months. Abiding by Patidar clan traditions, his mother had taken him to her family's ancestral home in Dangarva during her pregnancy. Bhogi was slowly coming to realize an unpleasant truth, that all the attention of the elders of the family was diverted wholly towards this new baby who did nothing more than sleep, cry, or cling to his mother's breasts, depriving Bhogi of his share of love. Bhogi, worn out and sleepy from a day spent playing outside with other kids, immediately fell into an exhausted sleep. It had hardly been half an hour when suddenly a piercing shriek came from the living room. It sounded like his mother's voice.

'No, this can't be true! No! No!' Kashi kept crying aloud.

Whatever had caused his mother to become so distraught was far beyond Bhogi's comprehension, but he was aware that it must have been something very frightening since everybody in the house immediately woke up. In no time, the family was joined by a swarm of neighbours who rapidly banded together after hearing the disturbing scream.

'Oh God! You cannot do this to me again. I have two young children. How will I raise them?' Kashi kept crying and beat her hands on her chest. Other women tried to hold her hands and calm her down.

Bhogi was completely lost and bewildered. For the life of him, he could not understand what such a fuss was being made about. Why were all the women weeping? He watched bemused as his mother, aunt and all the other females retired to their inner chambers to don black clothing and began beating their chests and crying out loud.

Within a few hours, Bhogi's cousin Ranchhod arrived from Detroj. Why, whatever was he doing here, especially at this time of the night? The home had taken on a grim air. His uncle Hari immediately assembled his bullock cart and somehow gathered two bulls available for rent before the sun rose. The entire family mounted the cart and set out in the wee hours of the morning, including a very confused four-year-old boy.

The stars gazing down upon him from the night sky were not accompanied by the moon that night, casting an unnaturally small amount of light onto the ground, inspiring a feeling of impending doom. Little Bhogi was still blissfully unaware that he would suffer the loss of his childhood before dawn broke.

As they passed through the village, the howling of dogs filled the air. It is said that dogs are able to sense the presence of Yamaraj, the Lord of Death, who arrives at the moment of the demise of any human. Even little Bhogi knew enough to be scared of such unbearable sounds. The bulls walked onward at a rapid pace, and an enduring silence fell on the bullock cart. Bhogi's fear mounted as he realized that his mother's tears were still pouring down her face. The only other time he had seen her weep like that was when his brother Bhikhu died. That incident had occurred a mere three years ago. Bhogi was still waiting for his brother's return.

He quietly asked, 'Mother, why is everyone so quiet?'

Kashi could only manage a pained whimper in response.

He then tried asking Hari.

'Don't worry Son; it was God's will,' Hari replied.

Bhogi still had no idea what exactly Hari meant, but he stopped asking.

The long stretch of dark road only amplified the feeling of foreboding in Bhogi that something bad was going to happen very soon, or had already happened. His mind was filled with anxiety and fear, not knowing that soon he would have no time and place even to bury his worries.

After four hours of arduous journeying down dusty paths under the light of the stars, the bullock cart finally reached Detroj. They arrived early in the morning and the mood was even more sombre than before. Bhogi's house was filled with people, all of whom were curiously dressed in white loin cloths with a swathe of cloth spread across their left shoulders. All the women had already donned white clothes and were beating their chests and swearing at Yamaraj for having taken away someone who was very dear to them. Bhogi's fears worsened as he started recalling similar happenings when Bhikhu was taken somewhere wrapped in white cloth, a journey from which his dear brother never returned. Bhailal had been with Bhogi for the entire night. He fervently searched his head. Who else could be missing? From amid that tangle of thoughts came one lucid one. Could it be his father?

Finally he gathered up the courage to ask Hari again. 'Is Father OK?' he timidly murmured.

Hari hung his head as he responded, 'Beta . . . your father . . . is in God's palace now.'

Little Bhogi thought he had lost everything in life. What he couldn't know then was that these were the first steps of a very long journey, one that would stretch for decades. At the time all he saw was his father, lying listless at the entrance of his house wrapped in plain white cloth with his mouth open. His face had some blood stains around it.

Kashi came and stood by her husband's feet, held them in her hands and began to weep with renewed vigour. Women from the neighbourhood as well as his aunts, including his favourite aunt Santok, came and started comforting her but beyond that there was no way to console her, no way to assuage that pain.

It had begun as a simple case of the sniffles. While at home, eagerly awaiting arrival of the newborn Bhailal, Mohanlal had caught a cold. Beyond a minor headache and a runny nose, he had no major illness. Soon though, he got a low fever and within a week the cold gave way to pneumonia. There were no doctors in the town. The barber, who doubled as a surgeon and healer, tried his best to help Mohanlal with herbal remedies. Instead of getting healed, Mohanlal's condition grew worse. Every night he was given clean pillows. By morning, the pillows were covered in blood and mucus from his painful cough. His condition worsened and he was no longer able to consume solid food, subsisting on only nimbu pani and biscuits. By the end of the week his fever-racked body finally gave up resistance, and he passed away. Luckily, the bloody traces the pneumonia had left had been cleaned before the arrival of his spouse and children.

Bhogi watched the funeral in awe and fear. Prior experience had taught him that once a person had been wrapped in white cloth, their return was not to be expected. Years had already passed and his younger brother had never come back. And now his father had decided to leave as well. Bhogi, still at a tender age, could only cling to his mother and cry. A village elder intervened and comforted Bhogi, telling him that his father had grown tired of waiting for Bhikhu and had decided to meet him. Now he was at least reassured that he had his mother and Bhailal to await his father and brother. He began to daydream about his family eventually becoming whole, with Bhikhu and Mohanlal returning to Bhailal, his mother and himself. His dream ended when he distantly heard Ranchhod's voice, telling him to get ready to leave for the samshan.

Bhogi finally realized that his father would not be coming back. He couldn't bear the thought of being separated from him. 'Let me go too. I want to go to God's house with him and Bhikhu,' he began. 'I'm sure he wouldn't mind me tagging along.'

Ranchhod only hugged him in response, whispering reassurances that did little to allay Bhogi's desperation.

Finally, he gave up and accompanied the funeral procession.

Bhogi sat next to his father's body. Four village elders and the priest applied ghee on Mohanlal's arms and feet. Then, the men of the village brought sticks and bamboos to the home. Within a few hours they constructed a long thin bier and lifted Mohanlal's body onto the makeshift bamboo bed. His head was covered with white cloth as well, and a small dried coconut was placed next to it. Then they wrapped a tight coir rope around the body, tying it snugly to the bamboo bed. Though concerned about how much the rope must have been hurting his father Bhogi decided to merely watch, thinking that the elders always did what was in the best interests of all. One of his uncles brought a copper jar filled to the brim with water from the Ganges river, which he had acquired a year before on a pilgrimage, and sprinkled drops of the holy water on Mohanlal's body, ensuring that his soul's transition would be smooth. Bhogi kept watching.

The bier was lifted by eight male relatives. Bhogi was hoisted atop the shoulders of one and was told to place a hand on the structure. He was asked to carry a dooni jar containing dried cakes of cow dung and straws, recently ignited, and emitting wispy smoke mixed with a pungent odour. Bhogi was at the front of the procession, alongside his uncle, followed by all the males of the village. The wailing women were left at home as a samshan was not a place where women were allowed to enter, unless dead. The procession slowly marched through the streets, all the while chanting 'Ram bolo bhai Ram'. Little Bhogi was too young to realize that each step toward the cemetery were bringing him closer and closer to the end of his innocence and childhood. As the procession reached street corners the pallbearers placed the body on the ground and, according to custom, changed the direction of the body on the bamboos. Finally, they reached the samshan and placed the bier onto a pyre of straw and bamboo.

Underneath the lone banyan tree the men stood in absolute silence, broken only by the screeching of crows and the priest's mantras. Without breaking the rhythm of the Sanskrit hymns, the priest handed a lit torch to Bhogi and the last rites for Mohanlal were chanted. When the priest was done, Bhogi, being the eldest son, was told to ignite the pyre with the torch, thus ending Mohanlal's saga.

The entire village was covered in a shroud of dull silence that morning. Mohanlal's father was very highly regarded in the village and his son had also been given his share of respect. His passing cast a dark shadow on Detroj. In those days, communities were more tightly knit than they are today. Fellow villagers were also close friends, and the passing of anyone made the whole village mourn.

The house was a scene of grief that entire day. All the women of the village were gathered together to support and help the ladies of the house. The men of the village were present as well, clad in white kurta-pyjamas, to pay their final respects to Mohanlal. The chaos frightened Bhogi and he too wept in distress. His mother beat her chest and wailed, while other women tried to console her and held back tears themselves. His aunt was in a similar state.

A Brahmin priest was waiting, and softly repeating

'*Na jayate mritaye va kadacin*
Nayam bhutva bhavita va na bhuyah,
Ajo nityah sasvato yam purano,
Aa hanyate hanyamane sarire.

'*Vedavinasinam nityam, ya enam ajam avyayam,*
Katham sa purusah partha, kam ghatayati hanti kam

'*Vasamsi jirnani yatha vihaya navani gihnati naro parani*
Thatha sarirani vihaya jirany, anyani samyati navani dehi

'*Nainam chindanti sastrani, nainam dahati pavakah,*
Na cainam kledayantyapo, na sosayati marutah

'*Acchedyo yam adahyo yam, akledyo sosya eva ca,*
nityah sarvagatah sthanur, acalo yam sanatanah,
avyakto yam acintyo yam, avikaryo yam ucyate,
tasmad evam viditvainam, nanusocitum arhasi

'*Atha cainam nityajatam, vityam va manyase mrtam,*
tathapi tvam mahabaho, nainam socitumarhasi

'*Jatasya hi dhruvo mrtyur, dhruvam janma mrtasya ca,*
tasmadapariharye rthe, na tvam socitumarhasi

'*Avyaktadini bhutani, vyaktamadhyani bharata,*
avyaktandhananyeva, tatra ka paridevana.'

'What is he saying?' Bhogi asked his uncle.

The priest overheard and gave Bhogi a sad, understanding smile. 'Beta, I am praying for your father's soul,' he explained. 'I am repeating a verse from the Bhagavad Gita. This is its meaning:

'Neither this, the embodied self, takes birth nor does it die at any time, nor, having been, will it again come not to be.

'This soul is birthless, eternal, perpetual and primeval. It is not slain when the body is slain. He who knows this, the indestructible, the eternal, the birthless, the imperishable qualities of the soul, grieves not for the demise of the physical body.

'As after casting away worn out garments, a man takes new ones, so after casting away worn out bodies, the embodied self encounters other, new ones.

'Weapons do not pierce this soul, fire does not burn the soul, water does not wet the soul, nor does the wind cause the soul to wither.

'This soul is eternal, all pervading, unmoving and primeval. It is said that this is unmanifested, unthinkable and unchanging. Therefore, once you have understood in this way, you should not mourn.

'Moreover, even if you think this to be eternally born or eternally dead, even then you should not mourn for this, Arjuna. For the born, death is certain. For the dead, there is certainly birth. Therefore, for this inevitable consequence, you should not mourn.

'The soul before life at its beginnings is unmanifested; it manifests after birth, and at the end of existence in this lifetime once again it becomes unmanifested. What complaint can there be over this?'

Bhogi understood little of what the priest said.

Hari then said, 'Beta, Mohanlal's soul is leaving his earthly body. He has gone to join Bhikhu, and is moving on.'

Bhogi still didn't understand fully, but it became apparent to him that his father too had been taken away from him.

6

Through Struggles to the Stars

'He who knows no hardships will know no hardihood. He who faces no calamity will need no courage. Mysterious though it is, the characteristics in human nature which we love best grow in a soil with a strong mixture of troubles.' – Henry Emerson Fosdick

Bhogi's entire world shifted on its heels. It was as if the future of everyone living in that tiny mud-brick house had died along with Mohanlal. Gone was the patriarch of the family. Gone was the only adult male in the household. And gone was any prospect that Bhogi ever had of a living a normal childhood.

Women never worked outside the home. The men took care, literally, of everything not involving cleaning, cooking and child-rearing. Mohanlal had been the family's sole provider after his brother had died. His grandfather, long since deceased, had given him all the tools that he would need to provide for the family. Mohanlal alone bore the responsibility of taking care of his mother, wife, two sons and his brother's widow and her two sons.

Now everyone was absolutely lost. Bhogi's two cousins were the oldest males in the household, but neither was even close to the age of shouldering the responsibilities that Mohanlal had carried out. Despite the grave amount of wear and tear on his body that had already been ravaged by a premature birth, a lifetime spent working in the sun and ill health, Mohanlal had managed to wake up early every morning and toil in the fields. But now there wasn't anyone who could do that.

After Bhikhu's death, the house had been in mourning for the loss of a loved one. Now, however, the house was in mourning for itself. Everyone realized that, barring a miracle, the road ahead was fraught with uncertainty and hardship, and the frightening possibility of more deaths.

Bhogi could read the fear in the eyes of every member of his family. He could see the anxiety behind the sad smile his mother bestowed upon him. He could sense the disquiet in Santok's reassuring words. He knew, just as well as everyone else in that house, that the struggles had just begun.

The village talati, who upheld the rules and regulations on behalf of the civil government, visited the family next day.

He was an Indian, but he liked to distinguish himself by upholding the stiff standards of the British. He knew quite well that he was nothing beyond a villager elevated by a little government authority but still austerely carried out his duties, expressing the typical formality of a British gentleman even when he spoke Gujarati.

'I know that this is a difficult time for you, and the last thing you'd want to be worried about is matters of protocol.' He waited for his words to sink in, and realized that the family had absolutely no idea what he was talking about. He continued coldly, addressing Kashi. 'Well, we have to discuss the matter of your husband's death and the passing on of his property. As you know, you have twelve acres of land that is tillable. It is up to me to ensure a smooth inheritance and make sure no one else stakes a claim.' When he still didn't get a response, he lost all pretence of propriety. 'Unless you pay me, you won't be getting any of the land that Mohanlal worked on.'

Kashi and Santok began to plead with him. 'Please Sir, see our situation. We are in no condition to offer anything. We have very meagre savings and have to take care of four children. Have some mercy.'

The talati was unmoved. 'If you don't ensure that I get a reasonable sum, you will soon be left with absolutely nothing.'

With no other recourse, they paid him half of the money they had remaining. With typical British composure, he bowed and left.

The family faced dire straits immediately thereafter.

Santok's two children realized that there was nothing left for their family in Detroj. Ranchhod had been in Ahmedabad during most of this episode. He begged his employer to allow him to return. He had already taken a leave of absence from his job and school to help the family get back to a normal life. Mangal was still in seventh grade, his final year at the local school in Detroj.

Bhogi noticed sudden changes in his mother's appearance after his father's death. She used to revel in wearing colourful clothes; now she only wore black like his aunt Santok. She had rubbed the vermilion off from her forehead. She had removed her mangalsutra, essentially removing everything that she had once worn with the pride of a happy bride. The ivory bangles, the only other jewellery that had been available to her, were taken off and stored in a makeshift safe, in the hope that she could pass them on to Bhogi's future wife.

Most painfully of all, Kashi had lost the perennially attractive smile that used to light up her face when she set eyes on Bhogi. Her face began to look as if it had been ravaged by decades of time, and her hair started turning grey.

After Mohanlal, there was no longer a breadwinner to till the fields. The ruthless talati had taken away much of what little money they had left. There were no men who would be able to sow the seeds for the crops, no men to hitch the buffaloes and plough the fields, no men to reap the harvest. To add fuel to the fire every single member of the family was already suffering from malnourishment, which was also something that had hastened Mohanlal's departure.

The family was at a loss. Between two widows and two children, with the eldest being four years old and the youngest barely twenty days, they couldn't make ends meet. Relatives, including Hari, stayed with them for a month. Following the tradition of Tadhi in Patel families, for the next month the fires that used to warm the traditional chula fire pit for cooking remained unlit. Neighbours and relatives brought food every day to allow the family to grieve together and come in terms with their loss. A ghee lamp was kept constantly burning to pay homage to and light the path for Mohanlal's soul.

Once the month of mourning was over, the family got together. Santok lit their chula again and began cooking khichhdi, the traditional Gujarati staple of rice and lentils cooked with oil and mustard seeds and served with buttermilk and onions. Santok served the meal to everyone. No one knew what to do next. It was as if everyone had lost the desire to live, or eat, or do anything. No one had the courage to speak. Santok took the first portion of food and fed Bhogi. She then held a small portion in front of Kashi's mouth, encouraging her to begin eating home-cooked meals again. Eventually, everyone finished their meal quietly and pensively.

Again there was silence. Ranchhod was eager to return to the city next morning as his employer had allowed him time off for just a month. Mangal was in a high school in a nearby village and had to go back to his boarding school soon. Hari was getting ready for a new season of crops and also needed to head back to Dangarva within the next few days.

Finally Ranchhod broke the silence. 'Kashi Ba, it is time to move beyond the mourning and grieving. I know that we have faced an unprecedented catastrophe. Our loss is irreparable. Mohanlal was like my own father. He took care of us. Without him, none of us would have survived up to this point. But now we need to secure a future for Bhogi and Bhailal, and we need to speak and work together. Just as Mohanlal was to me and Mangal, I will be to Bhogi and Bhailal. Together we will be able to survive as one family. I will bear Mohanlal's mantle, and I will lead the family out of this period of difficulty and misery.'

Santok realized that all the children had suddenly lost their childhood and matured into adults. Although sad, this was not new in villages; there were more than a few other families in Detroj where children had to take over the responsibilities of adults.

Pointing to Kashi, still silently grieving in the corner, Santok testily asked, 'How can she get beyond this point, Ranchhod? She has lost everything in her life. She is way too young to have to go through this. Don't you see she has a month-old baby and a child of four? She has a long way to go. You men will never understand what we go through as widows. She isn't fit to start working yet.'

Ranchhod knew he was treading dangerous ground, and diplomatically added, 'I do realize this, Ma. Please do not misunderstand me. At the same time, if we fall now, none of us will ever rise up again.'

He turned to Kashi and said, 'Kashi Ba, I understand your emotional state. But wasn't it you who showed strength when my father passed away some years ago? Without your encouragement and solace, we would not have been able to move on with our lives. That is the reason why Mangal and I have been able to carry on further studies and progressed in our lives. Look at Bhogi and Bhailal. They deserve a chance. Without all of us working together, neither of them will ever see a brighter light in their life.'

'I see your point, Ranchhod.' Santok acquiesced.

She slowly came forward and held Kashi's hands. 'I know your life is going to be different from now on. But you have to get your spirit together and move on, if only for the sake of the children.'

Kashi then began to voice her many anxieties: 'How will we feed ourselves, Ranchhod? We don't have any money. Whatever little savings we had in the form of grains and wheat, we had to barter for his treatment. The talati took half of what was left. None of us is capable of going out and tilling the land either.'

Santok looked at their buffaloes. She had an idea, and conveyed it to others. 'We still own two buffaloes. I am sure we will be able to milk them and produce enough butter and ghee that we can sell and support ourselves. We can also do some work at home for some extra money.'

'Work! Like what? I have never worked in my father's house. It is below our dignity to do the work of lower-caste women!' Kashi screeched. Even poverty and widowhood weren't enough to shake the caste barriers that were so strictly drilled into her head. She then beseechingly looked at her brother Hari. He knew quite well what she wanted from him.

Hari slowly said, 'Kashi, you know that my family is blessed with more than we need. I personally would be very happy to support you and your children and have you move in with us. However, you also know society and elders will not approve. After your marriage, your place is permanently here in Detroj. If you move away and join us, we will all be outcastes in the Patidar samaj.' He paused briefly to allow his words to sink in. 'You also know that our elder brother Somalal is the president of the Patidar Samaj in eighty-four villages. He and the other elders define and write the rules for the appropriate behaviour worthy of our caste and samaj. If you do not follow what they have prescribed for widows, then who else will? I'm sorry, but in this matter I have to support Somalal.'

Kashi looked outside. The sun was already sinking below the horizon, and all the buffaloes had headed back from the outskirts of the village after grazing in the fields. Their hooves had disturbed the ground and the sky had grown hazy from the dust the herd had thrown up into the air. Kashi felt that her own future was becoming as hazy as the dusty sky. She was stung that her brother was willing to callously abandon her for the sake of her more influential elder brother.

Santok nudged her to look at her children's faces. They appeared weak and malnourished. Kashi instantly understood what she was trying to convey.

'OK,' Kashi said. 'What if we get kala from the merchant's shop and work at home? We can separate cotton from the seeds, sell the cotton seeds and get paid. I know for a fact that Chanchal does it every day. She said that she was getting paid good money for it. And more importantly, it isn't the degrading work of the shudras.'

After seeing her poor children's faces, maternal love quickly conquered all of Kashi's ego and reservations. She was ready to put aside her pride and start supporting the family.

'I too will help whenever I can!' Mangal joined in. Both Kashi and Santok had smiles on their faces. Not knowing what Mangal meant, Bhogi, who didn't want to be left out, added, 'I will help too!'

Tears rolled down Kashi's eyes as she heard this. She realized that when she was a child she used to talk about toys and playing, but her poor son had to start talking about working just so that his family could stay afloat.

Widowhood was very common in that era. Although women were relegated to household matters and not allowed to gain education or knowledge of anything outside the household realm, society had still managed to create a number of ways to allow them to continue living. The Patel family had decided to shed their weakness and despair, and move on with life. They realized that their buffaloes were by no means paltry assets. These two animals would, for years to come, prove to be the primary means for the widows to make a living and provide for their children.

Santok began to step-up her earlier role in the daily chores. Now, every morning she utilized more milk to make ghee. Although the children occasionally had to forgo their share of milk in the mornings, they would at least be able to survive. The boys wandered around the neighbourhood every day, selling ghee and milk to the other villagers and, in this way, earned a pittance that allowed them to continue surviving.

They also earned money by picking cotton pods, then known as kala. This job had been traditionally reserved for widows. Merchants purchased the kala fruits of the cotton plant from farmers who grew them across the village, and kept them at their shops to be picked up in the mornings by widows or their children.

Each morning, everyone in the Patel household picked approximately a kilo of cotton from the kalas. The boys then took the picked cotton to the merchant who took them to the local factory that contained the only cotton gin in the village. There, the merchant sold the cotton and gave Bhogi and Mangal the commission the family was owed for completing the labour.

The kala-picking actually served a dual purpose. After the cotton was picked out, the remainder of the fruit was relatively easy to ignite and burned for a significant amount of time. Therefore, after the cotton had been sold by the merchant, the boys bargained and sold the kala peelings to the owner of the steam-powered cotton gin, who used them to power his factory as kalas were a cheaper alternative to charcoal.

The family owned a total of twelve acres of land spread out in single-acre pieces across the village outskirts. Some of these acres were barren wastes of sand and grew nothing outside of nuts, while others were immensely fertile. After Mohanlal's demise, the full capability of these fields was never going to be utilized again. The women were incapable of ploughing; they lacked both the muscle and the willpower. The children were far too young to be able to plough an entire field by themselves. Selling the land was unheard of. Those twelve acres had been passed down for generations and would be sold only as a last resort. Instead, they loaned out the land to a family of thakores –individuals who made their living as small-scale sharecroppers. Typically operating on plots of land that were, for one reason or another untillable by the owners, thakores made a temporary home on a piece of land owned by another and sowed and tilled the land using their own tools. When the crop finally grew, the thakores kept half of what had been grown and the land owners took the other half. This arrangement was made with a thakore's family by Kashi herself and, combined with the kalas and ghee, it would help the family to survive.

In this way, every day passed in relative monotony, beginning with milking and kala-picking and ending with visits to the cotton gin factory. Nights, on the other hand, were a frightening prospect. Detroj was an isolated village. Few ventured out late at night. In fact, the last time people in the Patel family had left home at night was when little Bhogi had made his excursion to the samshan. The noises of wild animals filled the night. Ever so often, the distant howling of a lone Indian wolf found its way through the shuttered windows of the house, intermingled with the frequent screech of a rowdy monkey roused from its sleep. Still worse were the ominous hoots of owls, then considered horrid portents of doom and evil. It was a sound that was believed to herald the appearance of thieves, dacoits and ghosts, and was always prevalent during the long hours after dusk. Every night it caused jarring fears to creep into the lonely household, especially since no adult male was present to protect the family. The barking of aroused street dogs was a common phenomenon as well, but often the more pitiable sound of a dog howling reached their ears and disrupted their sleep, putting doubt and panic into the minds of the family, for it was believed that a dog wailing meant the imminent death of someone dear to the one who heard the cry. Every time this sound filtered into the home, a damper was immediately put on conversation and sleeping heads turned worriedly, with everyone fervently praying and hoping that they wouldn't lose another loved one.

Bhogi's social life suffered another setback. Now that his father had died, the neighbourhood bullies found him an easier target. The gang of children was led by Jeevan, an eight-year-old power broker. At a young age, he had already attained a pot belly and was known for being lazy and spoiled. He was also the son of a money-lender, which made his family quite wealthy. Despite his chubby cheeks and jovial appearance, his eyes retained a look of shrewdness and cruelty. While harmless himself, he was constantly accompanied by Babu and Soma, his tall and muscular yet idiotic and almost troll-like cronies. These three were the leaders of the neighbourhood boys. Whenever Jeevan picked on Bhogi, one of his favourite victims, the others followed suit.

'Hey, here comes Bhogi the bhikari,' Jeevan usually began, calling Bhogi a beggar. The others would jeer too.

'Why don't you go back to your mother and father?'

'That's because he doesn't have a father!'

'Well, he can always try to get his big brother and come after us.'

'No, he doesn't have one of those either!'

Finally, tired of coming home day after day in tears, Bhogi stopped even trying to play with the neighbourhood children and became a recluse. This didn't stop them from harassing him.

One day, Ranchhod happened to pass by when the bullies were picking on Bhogi. Hearing the crude remarks aimed at the four-year-old, Ranchhod became enraged. He grabbed Jeevan by the collar and dragged him through the dirt-covered streets of Detroj to his father, Shantilal the bania. Ranchhod smacked Jeevan hard on his face twice, right in front of his father, and told Shantilal what had happened.

Although he was livid at the way Ranchhod was beating his child, Shantilal was still a businessman to the core. He knew that his livelihood depended on lending money to illiterate farmers and then living off the interest. Above all, Mohanlal's family had always had the reputation of being honest and reliable, and the father's passing had only made them more promising clients. Shantilal couldn't risk alienating such a lucrative contact; he anticipated that without a father to bring in money, Ranchhod would soon come to him for money. And Ranchhod, as a city dweller, invited particular interest. Despite wages not being high, the perception in the village was that everyone who went to the city would eventually come back rich. Shantilal couldn't afford to confront Ranchhod.

For the sake of appearances, he yelled at his son and added a few more slaps for good measure. Jeevan went away crying. Shantilal apologized to Bhogi and Ranchhod. This was the first time Bhogi felt that he could raise his head and carry himself properly. He also saw that living in a big city accorded his brother special status in the village. He decided to seek his own opportunity for migrating to Ahmedabad one day and becoming as respected as his cousin Ranchhod.

One way or another, the widows managed to survive and allow their children to keep moving on in life. Ignoring her hardships, Kashi insisted that each of them attend school when the time came. Even though this meant more work for them, Kashi and Santok were willing to make that sacrifice to ensure that their children made a better life for themselves. They managed to send Mangal to the boarding school in Kadi, where he spent three years. He had few months to go before his schooling was over.

In the spring of 1940, Mangal came home for Holi, the festival of spring. He looked anxious and was quiet during most of the festivities. Finally, before going to his khatlo, he brought up the reason.

'Mother, Aunty, I want to tell you . . .' he began hesitantly.

'Yes, Son?' Santok asked.

'I want to go to Ahmedabad for college.'

The response was just what he had expected, and far from what he wanted. 'You have responsibilities here!' Santok yelled. 'What do you think you're going to do with college education? Education beyond high school is meant for zamindars and banias. As far as we are concerned, all that matters is to be able to count and understand basic maths so that no one can fool us.'

Mangal, however, wasn't one to be cowed. He had prepared himself for this. 'Ma,' he asserted, 'I want to study to become a teacher. Isn't Ranchhod already in Ahmedabad?'

'Don't bring him into this. Your brother is old enough to pursue his follies, but I will not let you follow him!'

Kashi added her voice to Santok's protest by exclaiming, 'There's no need for higher education and teaching! Remember, you are a poor farmer's son. That is what our ancestors did for all these generations, and this is where your destiny also lies. No one in our family ever went beyond high school but for Ranchhod. And do you see where he is now? Always in the city; never at home. Is that what you want too?'

Mangal refused to give in. He continued, 'That is precisely why I want to break this cycle. Look at you both. You are intelligent and dedicated, and yet every single day you keep doing manual labour! I'm sorry but I can no longer see you picking cotton for the rest of your life. I want to see you live a life where you do not need to work any more. And, above all, I don't want my children to lose their childhood and have to bury the simplest pleasures for the sake of survival.'

Tears started flowing from Mangal's eyes as he recalled the damage done to Bhogi's innocence by his family's poverty.

'Mangal, enough is enough,' Santok interjected. 'I know how much you would like to study and help us. But we need someone to look after our land as well. Once you take up a plough, everything will be fine. We will be able to make some more money and none of us would need to do labour work any more. Picking up a plough doesn't need fancy books or graduating. Your place is at home. We did let you complete your high school. We don't have the money to pay for your college education anyway! You know we have land that we need to start cultivating.'

'Would you let me go if I manage to pay for my tuition?' Mangal asked perceptively. He knew what was bothering his mother and aunt the most.

Both Kashi and Santok had tears in their eyes. They realized how desperate Mangal was to continue his studies. They were not against his progress and neither did they want to stand in the way of his education. But they were apprehensive of losing him. They had both lost their husbands. Ranchhod had already left the village and was practically living in the city. In their minds, Mangal was too tender to leave Detroj and find his feet in Ahmedabad. Also, there were exorbitant expenses involved. At the same time, they also knew that he did not want to go for himself. He wanted to sacrifice the relative ease and familiarity of life with his family in Detroj for securing a brighter future for them.

Reluctantly, both the women gave Mangal permission to go with the condition that he would return upon completion of his college studies.

Bhogi continued to help his mother and aunt in Detroj while his two elder cousins paved their way for the future through higher education. He also had the responsibility of helping raise Bhailal. Bhogi began each day long before dawn when he led the buffaloes out to graze before making his way to school. He returned home not to his school books like other children did, but to the buffaloes and buckets of ghee that needed to be sold. Finally when night fell, he sat outside, straining his eyes under the soft glow of a kerosene lamp, so that he could study and catch up with what the rest of the students did during the day.

In this manner, time passed. Both Ranchhod and Mangal finished their education and found jobs. Ranchhod was hired as a physical education teacher in Ahmedabad and Mangal got work in a cloth mill. They both started urging Kashi to send Bhogi to the city for higher education, which would allow him to make a good career, instead of tending buffaloes and backbreaking farming for an entire lifetime. Kashi, still wounded by the loss of her husband, absolutely refused to let her eldest son out of the village. It would take a drastic event to do so. And yet, for better or for worse, such an event ended up occurring.

It was 1945, and the British presence in India was now greater than ever. World War II had just ended, with the Allied armies coming out triumphant. Turbaned Indian sepoys of the Royal Army were a frequent sight, and would occasionally halt at people's homes to drink water during their long journeys through the perennially parched lands of northern Gujarat. The officers of the Raj never forgot to stop by the village granaries and insist on their taxes and tributes. Their grip on the village was as firm as it had ever been, and a percentage of all the crops a farmer harvested was given to the merchants who duly paid the British officials when they came calling. For the past year, rainfall had been scarce and the crop was minimal. At a great personal loss, the merchant in Detroj did not collect the complete tax from the villagers but paid with whatever grains he still had in his granaries, which was still far from the full amount. The villagers nervously awaited the arrival of the district official. On the fateful night of 24 June, an event would take place that would prove to be the catalyst for Bhogi's future.

The freedom movement had reached its zenith by then. The masses of India were moving in a united wave, with Mahatma Gandhi as their head. Savage beatings, arrests, and even the Jallianwala Bagh massacre, did not dent the movement. Detroj had always been in staunch support of Gandhi; he had even come to the village some years earlier.

Bhogi's uncles, Hari and Somalal in particular, were highly involved in the freedom struggle. They came to Detroj and convinced the merchant and the rest of the villagers to take a stand against the British. Poor monsoon ensured that unless they starved themselves, they wouldn't be able to pay the tax. They decided to hold a protest by having the village elders collectively refuse to pay their annual tax on behalf of Detroj.

All the villagers gathered in the centre of Detroj as they sent an individual to inform the local government official of their decision. On the evening of the protest, the wealthy zamindar of the region hosted a party at his colossal mansion in one of his many farmhouse estates, located 100km from Detroj. An invitation typically meant that one had a high government position in the Raj or owned thousands of acres of land. The party was the perfect picture of wealthy debauchery, where the only thing that flowed faster than the liquor were the rupee notes that the distinguished 'gentlemen' tossed at barely clothed dancers. The party lasted until the wee hours of the morning, when drunken sahibs stumbled to their vehicles and rudely ordered their chauffeurs to take them home. One of the attendees was none other than the British district official of the Indian Civil Service, in charge of collecting taxes for the region.

Inspired by Gandhi, all the residents of Detroj had gathered in protest against paying the tax as part of the non-cooperation movement. Children and adults alike elected to take out a procession and chant slogans against the tyranny of the British empire. Bhogi joined in, chanting, 'Takli nahi to teer chhe, Gandhi amaro veer chhe!' If not with the spinning wheel, we will win freedom with the arrow. Gandhi is our hero.

The local representative, irritated by these slogans, ordered the arrest of some twenty-odd people, including adults and children, one of whom was Bhogi. Police officers started beating the rest of the villagers with lathis.

Meanwhile, the representative received the message that the villagers had refused to pay any of their taxes and immediately sent word to the official. Worried that neighbouring villages would soon follow the example of Detroj, the representative was determined to interrupt the ICS officer's night of revelry and informed him of the goings-on in the middle of the party. Already in a bad mood at having his fun interrupted, the intoxicated official decided that he had to make an appearance at Detroj and bully its residents into compliance. He called for his car and stumbled in, directing the chauffeur to Detroj. Upon arriving at the village early the next morning, however, the official was still in no state whatsoever to conduct any sort of official business. The chauffeur then summoned the villagers.

Kashi, worried about Bhogi's arrest, started pleading before the ICS officer. Still under the influence of alcohol, the official promptly vomited out the excess gin he had consumed over the past twenty-four hours. In his drunken state of arrogance, he began to call in broken Gujarati for 'water, if the savages had ever heard of cups'. As his chauffeur politely requested that Kashi bring some water for the sahib to drink, the sahib himself stared around the village with undisguised disdain for a life that he viewed as 'uncouth'. When Kashi nervously brought the water, she pleaded with the sahib to release her son.

He yelled at Kashi and spat at her feet, screaming, 'You rayats will never know anything beyond a life as donkeys. Every cent you earn we will take in tax. You can't read or write or even speak a civilized language, and will never go beyond this shithole you call a house! Even the idiotic sahukars are better off!'

Rayat was an extremely offensive word for the poor citizens of India, and the sahukars were the merchants of the bania caste. In that one sentence, the official had summed up the British Raj's opinion of India in that era: a land of many intolerable peasants and a few rich tolerable (and anglicized) gentlemen. Hearing this abusive language, the village men started assembling in front of the officer's car. It was clear that if he continued in this manner, the consequences would be grave. No resident of Detroj would allow a lone widow to be insulted, even by a high ranking British official. Sensing the storm that was gathering around him and fearing the repercussions if the crowd got out of control the chauffeur, profusely apologizing, manoeuvred the still babbling official into the car and drove off.

Bhogi was released with others. Detroj never paid the tax, and the official didn't make a repeat visit.

This incident made Kashi realize the partial truth behind the harsh words of the official. She couldn't sleep the whole night.

She kept looking blankly at the starry sky as if wanting her deceased husband Mohanlal to come and guide her in doing what was best for Bhogi and his younger brother.

'Are you OK, Ma?' Bhogi suddenly asked.

'What are you doing? Aren't you asleep yet? You have a busy day ahead. You have to feed the buffaloes, get kalas for Santok and me, and then go to school. Go back to sleep.' Kashi pretended to hide her anxieties and concerns.

'I'm sorry that you had to listen to abusive language from that white sahib. I just got carried away with the crowd. Even our teachers at school have been inspiring us to rise up against the sahiblog. I promise I will never do anything without asking you. Will you forgive me now?' Bhogi was genuinely apologetic. He felt that he had let his mother down by leading the group of children against the British tyrants.

'Oh no, Beta. I am not upset with you. In fact, quite the opposite, I am so proud of you. The whole village was talking about your bravery yesterday. Today I realized that you will make our family's name shine in the world one day. I'm just worried about something else.'

'What is it? You always say that between you and me, we can face the whole world. We have faced tragedies unlike anyone else. What is bothering you now?' Bhogi sat up in his khatlo. The sky was still dark and, except the distant yowling of hounds and foxes, only Bhogi's and Kashi's voices could be heard

Kashi got off her khaatlo and hugged her son. Although Bhogi could not see her face, he could feel the tears rolling down her cheeks.

'I want to send you to Ahmedabad.' Kashi finally said. 'I want you to study in the high school and become a big sahib so that no one will ever scream at your wife. I felt so helpless in front of everyone and the dirty stinking gora sahib. The only reason he could yell at me was because we are poor illiterate farmers, and they treat us like animals. I was happy that the whole village had gathered and that sahib had to run away. But what if no one had come to help us?'

'But Ma! Weren't you upset with Mangal when he wanted to leave for the big city? I have also heard Santok Aunty complain about Ranchhod, about how he does not visit and that he has lost all his roots and attachment to Detroj. I don't want to do that. Who will help you bring kalas? Who will help you feed the gaurs? Who will do the calculations and read letters for our neighbours? Who will write letters and talk to the bania for our accounts? Who will look after Bhailal?'

Bhogi was not very keen to leave his hard-working mother and aunt at the mercy of the neighbours. He had found a unique and indispensable position among the neighbours. While Bhogi was not aware of the long-term consequences of remaining a farmer and looking after a family in the village, Kashi had lived through the hardships of that life. But even if he had understood, Bhogi would never have wanted to leave his mother to suffer all by herself. He was also very aware of the enormous expense involved in going to Ahmedabad for his education, and didn't want to burden his mother with any additional stress.

Without further education, though, Kashi knew that Bhogi would invariably be set to suffer the harsh lives of his forefathers, toiling for mere sustenance. He would always have to serve others, whether they were zamindars or British sahibs. She knew then and there that to fulfil his destiny, she would have to part from Bhogi and that he would have to acquire higher education. Tearfully, she explained to him that he would be joining Ranchhod in Ahmedabad and would be staying with him during the next school year. Bhogi, only twelve at the time, had no idea what this meant for his future.

Their conversation went on for the whole night. At the crack of dawn, Kashi asked Bhogi to write a letter to Ranchhod, asking him to come to Detroj as soon as possible. Reluctantly, Bhogi drafted the letter of his own exile.

Fortunately, both Ranchhod and Mangal were free to travel back to Detroj for a few days. Once they arrived, they planned Bhogi's departure for the city.

The arrangements to send Bhogi to Ahmedabad were completed within a month. Bhogi had been Kashi's life. For her and Santok, he was companion, mathematician and book-keeper all in one; he was their herdsman and counsellor. Bhogi had acquired a responsible temperament and demeanour at the tender age of twelve, which was rarely seen even in adults.

Ranchhod was determined that Bhogi be placed in the best school possible which, at the time, was C.N. Vidyalaya. However, it was a school full of affluent Indians, most of whom had been completely anglicized. It was also very expensive.

Mangal was aware of their limited financial resources. Educational loans didn't exist in India's economic dictionary. However, there was a slim possibility of financial help that Mangal had come to know about. He first discussed the expenditure involved.

'Is this school really that expensive?' Kashi sighed.

She considered her possessions, including her wedding gifts and ornaments; they weren't enough. Finally, she looked at the buffaloes and told Mangal about her own plans. 'I do not need any of these. Maybe Bhogi will be able to buy jewellery for his wife when he gets married. And we can perhaps sell the house as well . . . '

Mangal quickly intervened, 'I didn't mean to scare you, Kashi Ba. There is also a possibility that Bhogi can qualify for a scholarship that will pay for his lodging and tuition. You know how smart he is.'

'Whether he gets it or not Mangal, I do not want Bhogi to continue suffocating in this environment. If he doesn't get it, we will do whatever is necessary. When do they test for this scholarship?', Kashi was getting impatient.

'On 1 August. We will leave for Ahmedabad in two weeks,' Mangal replied.

Bhogi was listening to this conversation and was annoyed at how little control he had over where his life was going. He interrupted, 'Ma, I hate to shift to the city. However, I will make sure that I study hard and win the scholarship. Under no circumstances will I let you sell your priceless belongings. The buffaloes and the house? How can you even think about selling them? I will make sure that you are able to raise your head with pride and respect in society for all the sacrifices that you have made for us.'

For the first time since his father passed away, Kashi saw tears rolling down Bhogi's face.

Mangal gave Bhogi the specific details of the exam and the scholarship. It was available to anyone in the state who could secure 90 per cent in the examination, and it would cover mathematics, science and Gujarati. Bhogi started preparing hard. He regularly read until well past midnight. Since he didn't own enough textbooks, he got permission from the schoolmaster to stay back after school and use its meagre resources.

Ten days went by and the time for little Bhogi to leave his comfort zone arrived. Ahmedabad was 60km away, and Bhogi was going to take the train. As it happened, an elderly man in the village also had to visit Ahmedabad at the time; so it was decided that Bhogi would accompany him. A fairly corpulent female neighbour too had to make the journey to visit her son in the city. Of the three, only the old man had been there before and he was to make sure the other two got there safe. They set out to the nearest train station, which was a forty-five-minute walk away.

Kashi and Santok walked to the station with Bhogi to see him off. Bhogi was overcome with emotion as he left Kashi. She was his mother, friend and benefactor; she was everything to him. For the first time in his life, Bhogi was being separated from the people who loved him. With sudden fear he clung to his mother, pleading and begging her not to let him go. With tears in her eyes, Kashi bid him goodbye, saying, 'My beta Bhogi! I know how hard it is for you to go to the big city at such a tender age. I know the difficulties and hardships that you will be facing. I feel as if I am tearing apart a piece of my heart to bid you goodbye. However, for you and your future, I am placing a heavy stone over it and letting you go. Go on, and be successful. I will be very happy if you never came back to the village but became successful instead. I will sacrifice anything and everything for you.' She started sobbing inconsolably until the local train to Kadi arrived.

Their plan was to take the train to Kadi, where a connecting train to Ahmedabad would arrive a few hours later. However, when the train finally came, it was jam-packed. While Bhogi and the old man managed to squeeze in, the rotund woman was out of luck. So that they could stay together, they decided to hitch a ride to Kadi on a farmer's bullock cart instead.

On the way, the old man realized with shock that he had left his bag on the train that had departed. One of his friends luckily happened to work at the station in Kadi, so the old man sent a telegraph message to him telling him to pick up his bag when the train came to a halt. The threesome finally reached the station a few minutes before the train to Ahmedabad pulled in. In those years, the train typically halted there for at least an hour before moving ahead. The old man's friend had taken the bag to his house, which was a ten-minute walk from the station. So after getting Bhogi and the other woman onto the train, he went off to get his bag. However, in an odd stroke of bad luck, for the first time in months the train actually adhered to schedule. Just when the man came within sight of the station on his way back, the train chugged off, leaving one frustrated old man at the station and two nervous people on the train.

Bhogi and the woman had no idea at which station they were to disembark. Ahmedabad had two major stations: one for the suburban area outside the main, walled city and the other that was situated within the city. The two were supposed to wait until they reached the city, but they were unaware of this. They asked the man sitting next to them to tell them when they reached Ahmedabad. He told them so when they arrived at the suburban station at dawn, and the pair got off.

Ranchhod and the woman's relatives were left waiting at the main station, while the two were at the suburban station. The woman remembered her son's address, and began asking around where it was located. People pointed in the direction of the city and told them that they were about 12km away. They walked for almost six hours, after which they finally reached her son's home. Her son then took Bhogi to Ranchhod's house and, after a frightening ordeal, Bhogi finally arrived at his destination. The scholarship Bhogi was going to try and win would pay his education bills and provide a stipend equivalent to four rupees per month. Both Mangal and Ranchhod were unsure of him winning the scholarship and had already been pooling in the money they had saved from their jobs to help finance his school fees. After all, Bhogi had been educated in a one-room shack by a teacher who had never gone beyond high school himself. His competition would include wealthy city students who had been groomed since birth with private tutors and education in the topmost schools in the state; who were after the scholarship for the prestige it accorded, rather than the need.

However, Bhogi's family had underestimated his desire to win the scholarship. The examination was to be held on 1 August and it was only 24 June now. For the next month, Bhogi seldom emerged from the living room where he would be engrossed daily in the new textbooks Mangal had brought for him from the school where he taught. Mangal and Ranchhod wistfully smiled during dinner when Bhogi spoke of how he would win the scholarship and make them all proud.

Finally, the day of the examination came and, after eating a hearty breakfast, Bhogi took a ride with Ranchhod on his old bicycle to the hall where the exam was to be held. As he drew near, he saw children in crisp, freshly ironed shirts and pants, stepping out of rickshaws and a select few coming out of their fathers' gleaming cars. As Ranchhod let Bhogi down, in his old handed-down shirt, he had no doubt that Bhogi would fail. There was simply no way a village boy could compete with the children he saw entering the examination hall.

And yet, when the results came out, Bhogi scored 92 per cent and won the scholarship. That night Ranchhod and Mangal took him out for dinner to celebrate. Bhogi was supposed to go back to Detroj within a week to wrap up the small business operation of the kalas, buffaloes and land lease. He had mixed emotions about leaving behind his mother and aunt back in the village to keep toiling, while he joined his cousins in Ahmedabad to enjoy the city life. The celebrations and happiness would last only for one night . . . .

7

Darkness Falls

'Nothing happens by chance, my friend . . . No such thing as luck. A meaning behind every little thing, and such a meaning behind this. Part for you, part for me, may not see it all real clear right now, but we will, before long.' – Richard Bach

With Bhogi gone Kashi began to feed Kalio, his now immensely aged canine friend. After a while, she even took it into her home and it provided her solace for the absence of her dearest son. Her daily routine had become quite mundane. Which is why when her sister-in-law became pregnant, Kashi decided to go and help her deliver the baby. She took Kalio with her to Dangarva where her brother lived.

The baby came out healthy, but Kashi did not.

While she was there, Kashi developed occasional sneezing and a slight cough. While both she and her brothers shrugged off these symptoms, they didn't stay mild for very long and soon gave way to raging pneumonia.

'Please get my Bhogi here. Please don't let me die. I want to see Bhogi. The poor child never wanted to leave me in the first place. Please do something.' Kashi continually sobbed.

She kept her hands folded as if she was praying to God and constantly looked at the sky covered with the dark, thick clouds of monsoon. Thunder and lightning only added to her anxiety and illness. She started shivering. Her body was writhing from a burning fever and soon she started spitting rusty-looking blood-soaked phlegm from her lungs.

Kashi saw this and remembered what she had been told of her husband's last days of illness before his death. She sensed that whatever had taken him away had now come back for her. 'No, no, this cannot happen to me,' she said to herself as she slipped in and out of delirium. 'I need to live to help Bhogi grow up. The poor boy has had everything snatched away from him. Not any more, please!'

Kashi's brother could do little to relieve her anguish. They called for the barber-surgeon. He arrived quickly but, shaking his head, only said, 'This is beyond my skill to heal. Far beyond my skill!' Armed with nothing more than his rudimentary surgical skills and a few old scalpels, there was absolutely nothing that he could do to halt the progression of the disease.

With frightening similarity to what had happened years before to Mohanlal, Kashi began coughing blood regularly and her condition rapidly worsened.

One of Mangal's friends in Ahmedabad was a doctor fresh out of residency, so he and Ranchhod went to him for help. The doctor was a kind man, who had been raised in a village himself. He assented at once and reassured them, 'Of course, I'd be glad to help. What are her symptoms?'

Ranchhod listed them: 'It started off as a mild cough, but soon became deeper. Then she started coughing rust-coloured mucus, and yesterday coughed up blood. She also has chest pains, high fever, and is constantly shaking with chills.'

'Oh my God, it could be pneumonia,' said the doctor. 'We have to get there as soon as possible.'

He immediately agreed to make the journey to the village and treat Kashi. There was no time to bother with trains, so Ranchhod and Mangal hired an old army jeep and a driver to take them there. Mangal, accompanied by Bhogi and the doctor, climbed into the jeep and pleaded with the driver to hurry. They had sent a telegram that help was on the way and that Bhogi was coming along with his cousin and a real doctor by jeep.

Kashi's condition was deteriorating every hour. She was surrounded by her brother's family, all praying to God to help keep her alive. After expelling a tremendous amount of blood in her last bout of coughing, her breathing slowed down and became more laboured. The severe pain in her chest worsened, but despite the agony in her ribcage she couldn't stop coughing. Her skin was scalding-hot to the touch and the shivering was uncontrollable.

When she was told that Bhogi was coming with Mangal and a doctor, Kashi had hope. She calmly said, 'My Bhogi is on his way to take me to the city for further treatment. From now on, I do not need to worry. He will come and get me. All my prayers for his life have been answered. I will sell my house and buffaloes for his studies, but will not let him come back to the village.'

As her delirium worsened, Kashi could only mumble Bhogi's name every few seconds. After a sudden spell of rapid breathing and dreadful shivering, her breathing suddenly started to slow down and her fever subsided too.

Just when her brother was about to yell with joy and thank God for answering his prayers, he noticed something else. Her nails had started to turn light-blue, followed closely by her hands, wrists and forearms. After the rapid shallow breaths earlier, Kashi could barely manage to breathe now. And yet, she kept saying, 'My Bhogi will be here soon . . . ' Her breathing soon slowed to the point where she could draw air only once or twice a minute. Her whole body was now turning blue. Her eyes were barely open and her body was ice-cold.

She finally worked up her remaining strength and whispered, 'Tell Bhogi I love him, and that he is going to make me proud.'

Kashi then closed her eyes, and her breathing came to a stop.

As Kashi was passing away, the jeep carrying Bhogi, Mangal and the doctor was being slapped right and left by a monsoon in its full fury. The sky was covered with dark clouds, giving the air an ominous sense of impending calamity. Torrential rain began pouring down minutes after they had left Ahmedabad. There were still no paved roads outside the cities and the jeep had to journey through dirt tracks to reach the destination. All four people in the jeep were thoroughly soaked within the first half hour. The rainfall turned the dirt roads into treacherous mud pits. It was almost impossible to make progress. Every other kilometre, the jeep got stuck either in the mud or in ruts along the road and the four would have to disembark and push with all their might until the vehicle became free again.

In this manner, the drive became longer and longer, with the doctor, driver and Mangal taking turns at the wheel. The water level kept rising the entire time to the point where the small dirt road became so difficult to navigate that the driver refused to go on. They had to stop in a village for almost the entire night before resuming their journey.

Bhogi, unaware of the distances, asked Mangal, 'How long is it going to be before we can reach Mother?'

Frustrated, Mangal replied, 'The rain gods are not favouring us. We could have made it there within three hours if we had roads like Ahmedabad or if it didn't rain like this.'

Bhogi folded his hands, looked up at the sky and started praying, with tears rolling down his cheeks. 'Oh Lord Indra,' he pleaded, 'the mightiest of the mighty rain God. Have mercy on us. I want to reach my mother so that I can bring a smile to her face. I have not seen her really smile since my father came to live up with you in heaven. For the first time I have reason to make her smile. Please have mercy on me, God.'

Even Mangal, the doctor and the driver had tears in their eyes upon seeing the despair on Bhogi's pitiable face. They all joined in his prayers. Bhogi kept weeping and praying. Slowly, they saw the clouds parting and a deep-blue sky finally emerged from behind the dark clouds. However, the damage was done. The roads were as bad as before, and it took several more hours before they made it to Dangarva. What should have been a three-hour journey took them a day and a half.

They finally arrived at Kashi's brother's home. As they hustled inside, each breathlessly explained why they were so late. In their eagerness, they didn't notice the downcast faces all around. No one had the strength to tell them what had transpired until the doctor, suddenly realizing the truth, asked where Kashi was.

Tearfully, her brother replied, 'She has moved on.'

Kashi had succumbed to her illness barely two hours before their arrival, never knowing that her fervent prayers of the past months for Bhogi's success in his studies had been answered. With her love for Bhogi being the last thing on her lips, she had passed away.

Bhogi was in shock. He numbly sat down, not paying heed to anything. For the first time he was faced with the full, awful impact of death. When his older brother and father had died, he had not been truly aware of the implications of death. Now, however, he was faced with the raw truth – that he would never again return home to his mother's comforting smile or her warm hug.

He didn't say a word until he overheard a whispered discussion between the doctor and the family members. The doctor told them that he might have been able to save Kashi had he arrived earlier. An antibiotic infusion that he had come prepared with in his kit could have saved her life. Bhogi began to weep uncontrollably, screaming curses at Mother Nature for the rain that had clogged the roads.

That night, when everyone else was asleep, Bhogi lay awake. Mangal's words kept repeating themselves in his mind. 'We could have made it there within three hours if we had roads like Ahmedabad or if it didn't rain like this . . . We could have made it there within three hours . . . We could have made it there within three hours . . . '

Bhogi made a vow to himself that one day, he would make rural roads just like the city ones and ensure that no one else died because of a rain storm.

Kashi's body was wrapped in cloth, except that it was red in colour since she was a woman. Her face was left uncovered and coconuts were placed around it. Bhogi was not allowed to see the body being wrapped. He silently sat outside the room where his mother's body was being prepared for cremation. His only solace was in knowing that at least his mother had now gone to a place where she would no longer know pain. She had left for an eternal journey and would join Mohanlal and Bhikhu. Now he was all alone in this world to carry on the burden of death and devastation on his thin shoulders. He had his younger brother, who was more of a responsibility than help. Bhailal was still in Detroj and could not make it on time either due to poor roads or travel conditions.

The funeral procession started slowly from Hari's house towards the samshan. Instead of climbing on anyone else's shoulder, unlike during his father's funeral, Bhogi was solemnly walking at the head of the procession, chanting, 'Ram bolo bhai Ram.'

At the crossroads they stopped and changed the direction of her head before continuing, until they reached the samshan. Bhogi was walking mechanically. He had just let go of all of his thoughts, ideas and plans; they could have been of no more significance at that moment than a log floating in a lake.

How could he build any plans at the moment? The only thing he ever wanted to do was bring a smile to his mother's face; see her smile like she did before the tragedies of life turned her old and grey. He had worked hard for the results of the scholarship so that his mother could stand up in society with her head held high, confident that her son would make a name for himself. And now, everything was gone. In just two hours God had taken away any hope Bhogi had of ever seeing Kashi again. While he had won the battle of making his mother proud, he had lost the important war of having his mother alive.

Bhogi sat down in the samshan. The Brahmin chanted shlokas from the Bhagavad Gita that sounded familiar in pronunciation but not meaning. Any vestiges of childhood Bhogi had were now long gone, and his new life began here. The Brahmin handed the torch over to Bhogi and asked him to walk around the funeral pyre seven times, and then place the torch next to Kashi's right big toe. Bhogi robotically followed his instructions and felt as if he had almost left his own body, and was observing himself, as his arm went down and lit his mother's funeral pyre.

8

Out of the Frying Pan and into the Fire

'All the powers in the universe are already ours. It is we who have put our hands before our eyes and cry that it is dark.' – *Swami Vivekananda*

All his life, Bhogi had everything taken away from him. The awful reality of death finally hit him and he realized that the person who mattered the most to him was now gone. And just like when his father had passed away, he wasn't there to whisper a final goodbye or give a final embrace. His mother's death, however, left a desire that burned much longer and fiercer than Kashi's funeral pyre.

Bhogi realized there and then that prayers to the gods weren't enough to solve problems. No amount of begging on his part had convinced God to stop the rain and allow the life-saving antibiotics to reach Kashi. He turned his sorrow at Kashi's death into anger at the gods. He stopped going to temples.

One day, Ranchhod confronted him. He began, 'Bhogi, take heed. The gods are not to be trifled with. You think you will ever be successful without their blessings?'

Bhogi scoffed in response, 'What gods, Ranchhod? The gods that took my brother away from me before I was a toddler? The gods that took away my father before I was even five years old? The gods who wouldn't let us save my mother's life? Face it – they aren't ever going to help us.'

Ranchhod was shocked by Bhogi's sudden outburst. And although he disagreed with everything Bhogi said, he could come up with no argument against it. He shook his head and told Bhogi that he was heading down a dangerous road.

Some weeks later, Bhogi was walking down the street. He saw an old blind man who was waiting to cross to the other side. Bhogi walked up to him and said, 'Dadaji, hold my hand. I will take you across to the other side.' The old man thanked him for his kindness.

When they reached the other side, the man turned and said, 'Thank you, dear son. May the gods watch over you and bless you.'

Bhogi gave an irate snort in response and said, 'Thanks Dadaji, but I don't think I'll ever be counting on their fickle help.'

'Why do you hate the gods so much, Son? Do you think they have done you an injustice?'

'Yes, and a great deal too.'

The old man asked Bhogi to take him to a bench and said that if Bhogi wanted to talk about it, he would listen. Not having anything else to do that day, Bhogi agreed.

He began, 'Well Dadaji, my mother was very ill in Dangarva. We had the medicine and the doctor to save her, and we went to the village. The rain, however, flooded the roads. Our jeep got caught in the mud and it took a day and a half to complete a three-hour journey. My mother died in the meanwhile.'

The old man softly chuckled. This angered Bhogi. 'Oh, so you find my misfortune funny, do you? What kind of a pervert are you?'

The old man, still chuckling, said, 'No Son, I am not laughing at your misfortune. I am laughing because a long time ago, I was exactly like you.'

Bhogi responded, 'Well, you've obviously changed since then. What made you revert to the tomfoolery that is religion?'

'When I was just a few years older than you, I lived in a village with my parents. One day, my father had to go on a train to the city. It was the monsoon season. He forgot his bag at home, so I was sent on my bicycle to take it to him.

'On the way back, it started raining. My cycle got stuck in the mud, so I had to walk the rest of the way. By the time I reached, my father had missed his train and had to take one the next day. That train derailed in the middle of its journey. The largest body part they found of my father was his forearm, with his rudrakash still tied across it.

'Just like you, I was livid at the gods. Had it not rained that day, I would have reached with my father's bag and he would have boarded the train that day; not the doomed one the day after. I cursed the gods for the next three years, until I finally met a man who told me what I am about to tell you.'

Bhogi was intrigued. 'What did he tell you?'

'He asked me to look around the village and tell him what

most of the people did for a living,' the old man continued. 'I told him that they were all farmers. He then asked what is needed for crops to grow. I responded that seeds, good soil and rain were needed. He then quietly asked how many people would have suffered had the rain not fallen that day. I realized that I had been looking at the situation just as it had impacted me, from one perspective. Had I looked at it from an aerial perspective, I would have seen just how much harm my desire would have caused. If it hadn't rained, my father may have still been alive but hundreds of others wouldn't have been. Think about your situation too. While you were pleading with God to halt the rain, many others were pleading to allow the rain to continue. God couldn't sacrifice so many others to save one.'

Bhogi listened with rapt attention. He had never considered that perspective. After a pause, he asked, 'Well, what then is the point of ever praying since God is obviously never going to help us?'

The old man laughed again 'You're a tricky one. I will tell you a fable the man told me. One day, a traveller was going on a journey via bullock cart. Along the way, its wheels got stuck in the mud. He started moaning and praying to Hanuman for assistance, until Hanuman finally appeared. He said to the traveller, "I cannot help until you first put your shoulder behind your cart and push with all your might. If you don't try helping yourself, neither I nor any other God will be able to come to your aid."

'After this encounter I became a changed man. Despite coming from a very poor and uneducated family I studied and, with some stroke of luck, became a doctor. I cannot deny God's role in this; without the help of God, do you really believe any boy living in a poor village would ever be able to come to Ahmedabad and become a doctor? God saw that I was putting in effort, and He rewarded me. I am old and grey now and my eyes are weak from cataract, but I see the same potential in you.

'You say that you cursed the gods because the rain they invoked made the roads muddy. But it was men who made the roads so poorly that the rain washed them away. God didn't listen to your pleas to make the rain stop, because doing so would have caused harm to many others. Have you ever considered becoming a civil engineer and designing better roads yourself? God may not have listened to you when you asked to make the rain stop, but if you ask Him to give you strength and good luck so that you can study hard, become an engineer and improve the roads, I have absolutely zero doubt that He will listen and make all your aspirations come true. And don't you think that by taking action and saving people's lives by building better roads, you will obtain thousands of times the satisfaction you get by ridiculing people's faith in God?'

Bhogi was overwhelmed by the words. Everything the old man said made perfect sense to him. He chuckled and said, 'The man who told you all this must have been one of the wisest men in history.'

The old man laughed even louder in response and said, 'Well, I should think so! His name was Swami Vivekananda.'

That conversation would remain etched in Bhogi's mind for ever. He realized then that God was always there to help, but that He would only do so if one made the effort and took the initiative first. He renewed his faith in God and threw himself into his studies, now confident that he would succeed. He decided that after he became an engineer he would improve the roads of the countryside, so that others wouldn't have to suffer like his mother did.

As time passed, Bhogi managed to move on from the death of his mother. His years were spent in Ahmedabad with Ranchhod and Mangal, both of whom soon got married. He spent his summer vacations back home in Detroj with his brother and Aunt Santok.

Two years later India became an independent nation, though this did little to impact their lives or free them from taxation.

Mangal soon got a job of teaching literature at C.N. Vidyalay. Bhogi's admission was further secured by Mangal's position, in addition to his scholarship award.

His classmates included the sons of leading industrialists and mill owners; children who were set to inherit fortunes that to Bhogi seemed legendary. Owing to this, he was never very socially active. The students around him were arrogant about their privileged lifestyles; children who drove cars when half of India couldn't afford bicycles. They had been born with golden spoons in their mouths, and never had to worry about the hardships of life. On the other hand, Bhogi, while by now solidly middle class and nowhere near poverty, had already seen struggles in his lifetime that the others could never even fathom: worries about whether there would be food to eat at night or whether the buffaloes would survive another drought. Bhogi resented them for their frivolous attitudes, and never became involved in their social circles.

Ranchhod and Mangal saved every paisa possible and sent it to the family in the village, despite the costs of living in the city and the comparatively low salaries of school teachers. Santok, now accompanied by her mother-in-law Gnan, worked doubly hard. The family's guardian angels, the two buffaloes, were still alive and healthy and afforded them some income. Each summer Bhogi returned to Detroj, to Santok and Gnan Ba's home which was finally rebuilt with the family's help to include a proper roof and an additional room. The entire family lived in a now-extended home of 350 sq ft.

Post-independence, India was a lost nation to begin with. British colonists did not want India to progress. They had seen just how strong the might of 400 million Indians living in poverty was when they assembled with the banner of truth and non-violence under Gandhi's leadership and challenged the mightiest empire in the world. Indeed, this was the first British colony that was able to free itself without taking up arms and resorting to a bloody revolution. It was said that the sun never set on the empire. However, independent India was the beginning of the end of the British era as England was soon to be surpassed by many other nations in terms of both economic and military strength.

At the time of their departure, the British diplomats had slowly but steadily sowed the seeds of mistrust, insecurity and hatred between Hindus and Muslims. The two religions that had once lived side by side, through good and bad days could no longer see eye to eye. Worse, instead of freeing India to an independent democratic government, they handed it over to 600 maharajas who were to rule different provinces as their own mini empires so as to ensure that the nation would never unite or get beyond petty squabbling. If it wasn't for the rapid action of the post-independence government to bring all those small princely states under the banner of a unified India, the nation would have failed. But, as a result, many important developmental works that could have been undertaken to help the general population got delayed.

The first catastrophe came in the form of a natural disaster that affected not only the Patel family but millions of others throughout the state of Gujarat: the Gujarat Drought of 1950. Droughts were a relatively common occurrence in the dry lands of northern Gujarat and the citizens had learned to adjust to them. Despite significant hardship, most people made it out alive, though typically a few pounds skinnier. The year 1950, however, brought something much worse. That year, the dark rain clouds of the monsoon never graced the skies and the crop of virtually every farmer failed completely. Every morning farmers watched the sky, praying for Indra to shower them with the blessing of rain, to no avail.

The hot sun never seemed to abate, its unyielding rays unblocked by clouds. For months on end, it seemed that hell itself had descended on the villages of Gujarat. There was no water for humans or animals to drink. Carcasses of wild animals littered the ground. The rivers and ponds all dried up, and the ground itself became so parched that it developed cracks and fissures almost 6 inches deep. All the villagers and farmers were carrying out yagnas to please the rain gods and continually asked for forgiveness for whatever sins had caused the gods to hold back the rain. Drinking water was quickly becoming an expensive commodity.

Many of Bhogi's neighbours had started migrating out of Detroj in search for greener lands on which they could survive. Rumours were spreading that the nearby desert of Kutch was rapidly expanding and would eventually engulf all of Detroj and its surrounding areas in its insatiable maw. A great number of

Bhogi's peers had actually died while chasing mirages for the sake of finding water for their animals, mirages that only led them farther into the desert where they invariably lost their way and died. Jeevan was one of them.

Bhogi, Mangal and Ranchhod went to live in Detroj to help Santok and Gnan to tide over the terrible crisis. Neither Mangal nor Ranchhod were particularly keen on staying in the village, but they didn't want to leave Santok and Gnan Ba behind. One day, Ranchhod gathered the courage to ask Santok, 'Ma, how long do you want to keep suffering in poverty here? Please come with us to Ahmedabad. Between Mangal and me, we will be able to look after you.'

Santok, instead of replying, looked at Gnan and their buffaloes. Ranchhod knew what she was trying to convey.

'We certainly can take Gnan with us,' he added.

'What about our buffaloes? Can we bring them with us?'

Ranchhod stayed silent. Mangal then jumped in. 'We can send them to the animal welfare camp, where they can live for the rest of their lives.'

Santok exploded. 'Do you know what you are saying? Do you care about these animals? They have been with us for all these years. They have fed and nurtured us. You grew up drinking their milk. They are like your mother. Their parents were a part of our parents' lives, and now when they need us the most you want to just dump them? You have become totally selfish in the city! You do not know what these mute animals mean to us. I would rather die than be separated from them. Before even dreaming about taking them away, dump me in one of those desert pits so that the vultures can eat away every piece of meat from my body.'

Santok was furious at the lack of compassion and sympathy

her sons exhibited for their priceless companions who had been with them in good times and bad.

Bhogi was equally upset by their suggestion, and told Santok, 'I will stay with you to look after them, if Ranchhod and Mangal don't.'

Slowly, the discussion cooled off and Ranchhod profusely apologized for his disregard towards the two animals who were almost like family members.

In the days that followed, it became more and more difficult to survive. Food and drinking water vanished. Scouring through animal excreta for food grains, once an action reserved exclusively for the untouchable caste, became a necessity for even the most stuffy and upper-caste Brahmins. Any kind of food grain found anywhere was regarded to be a blessing.

Dogs fought over the smallest scraps of food. Rancid meat seemed to be the only food available; and many more animals died of diseases spread by the rotting meat that they were forced to eat.

At first, the vultures grew fat but soon the terrible weather took a toll on them as well. Even birds that preyed on death needed water to sustain their lives and soon enough, the bodies of vultures lay alongside the other animals they had once eagerly devoured.

One day, as he was walking with Ranchhod, Bhogi came across three famished wild dogs fighting over some sort of a dead animal. The two shooed it away and began approaching the carcass. Suddenly, Ranchhod saw what it actually was and quickly turned around. 'No, Bhogi, we have to go. We have to go now!' he exclaimed, trying to drag Bhogi away.

'What on earth could it be?' Bhogi curiously asked. 'What happened? Did the dogs leave a bloody mess behind? Come on, we've all seen these things lying around before. At least let me take a look at it.'

Ranchhod adamantly put his foot down and urged, 'Bhogi, I am older than you and I'm saying no. We have to go back.'

'Oh stop being such a stickler.' With this statement Bhogi shoved his cousin aside and, not heeding his entreaties, approached the body.

He promptly vomited. Ranchhod was trying to warn him that the body was of a dead human being.

Neither said anything on their way back. The sight had severely shocked Bhogi. He couldn't comprehend how the merciless weather was capable of taking human life along with the animals.

It was at this time that something else multiplied their troubles manifold. This problem was borne on a cloud.

From the village it appeared as if the gods had finally answered the prayers of the starving farmers begging for rain. Dark clouds appeared in the skies and blotted out the sun. It seemed that rain had finally arrived.

As the clouds came nearer, however, it became very obvious that they weren't bringing rain – they were bringing death.

What appeared to be rainclouds were really swarms of locusts. The millions of insects collectively blacked out the sun and darkened the sky. When they descended, they destroyed everything living in their path.

The clouds descended directly on Detroj and wreaked absolute havoc. Any living plant left in the area was wiped clean.

Bhogi was outside when the swarm descended. He couldn't see in any direction and madly flapped his arms about, killing many. But more just kept coming. Ranchhod ran outside and brought him in. Bhogi was disturbed for the next few hours.

When they went back outside, the scene was deathly quiet. The locusts had covered literally everything: houses, streets; even the buffaloes were moving frantically, trying to shake off the swarming insects. None of them had ever witnessed such a calamity before and it shook them to their very core.

The Brahmins proclaimed that the wrath of the gods had fallen on them and insisted that only through prayer could such a problem be lifted. However, prayer seemed to do little to alleviate the situation.

A few days later, however, the swarm simply picked up and moved on to the next village. In its wake, it left absolute devastation.

There was no greenery visible now. Whatever little plant life had made it through the drought was absolutely decimated by the waves of locusts. Trees had broken and fallen under the weight of thousands of angry locusts settling on their rapidly weakening branches. Even the entire railway system of northern Gujarat was shut down by the government after three horrific derailments. The train tracks were covered by countless locusts. As the trains ran, they crushed the locusts under their wheels. There were so many of them, however, that their blood covered and soaked the wheels and the tracks, making them so slick that trains would run right off of them. Many perished due to the locusts; even in death they proved to be tremendously lethal.

The drought had ensured that there was barely enough water to feed the family and the buffaloes, and absolutely none left to water the crops. Not that it mattered, since the locusts had destroyed whatever crops had grown anyway. Starvation wasn't a risk for the Patel household as the family had thoughtfully saved some extra grain from the more bountiful crop in the previous years just in case of such an emergency.

Unfortunately, not everyone was gifted with such foresight. Human bones lining the roads were no longer strange sights, as starvation became the biggest cause of death. The Patel household suffered from a different concern. While the family had enough to eat, by no means did they have enough to feed two enormous buffaloes. And if the buffaloes died, so would the family's income and ability to survive in the future.

Tired, worn out and depressed, Santok asked Bhogi, 'Beta, where shall we go to find some food for us and the buffaloes? They look emaciated. I am worried about them and us. Maybe we should have listened to Ranchhod and, instead of staying here in Detroj, moved to Ahmedabad.'

'Please do not talk like that Santok Aunty. These two buffaloes have been with us for over fifteen years. No matter how bad the situation got for us, they never thought of leaving. How can we think about abandoning them at such a time? They will die without us. Let me take a stroll in and around the fields and see if we can find something to eat. I also need to look for water somewhere.'

Without a real destination in mind Bhogi walked in the general direction of the samshan. Animal carcasses were lying everywhere. Thin, withered children were slowly walking around the carcasses looking for their excreta and seeing if they could locate some grains that could be used for their own consumption. As he approached the samshan, Bhogi saw that the cacti that grew there were still green and, to his surprise, the big banyan tree was still intact.

'How could this happen? How is it possible that when everything else has been destroyed by the locusts, this banyan tree is undamaged? Am I seeing some sort of a ghostly vision?' As he shook his head, Bhogi looked around and found the answer. Smoke that was still rising from the funeral pyres must have irritated the locusts, and ensured that they didn't destroy that refuge as well.

Bhogi slowly went back into the village. He didn't want to let anyone else know about his priceless discovery.

As he reached home, Santok was seriously considering putting the buffaloes out of their misery before they were affected by the agony of death by thirst. But Bhogi stopped her. 'No Santok Aunty. Please do not do that. I have a plan that could get us all food.'

'How? There is nothing left to eat or drink!'

Bhogi then described what he had seen at the saashan and told her his plan. The only plants that were still alive and standing were the cacti and other thorny, inedible species. What most people chose to do to survive was, with an enormous effort and a process that few today can still remember, convert the cacti through a great deal of mashing and soaking into something edible at least for animals. However, Bhogi's plan was more ingenious even though a tad morbid.

The enormous banyan tree had been spotted by people before Bhogi. Luckily for him, however, it carried a great deal of superstition. The tree was said to be haunted by the ghosts of those who hadn't been given last rites and were left to eternally meander in the samshan. Indeed, saying the word 'chalo' was not allowed there, for fear that the ghosts would hear and follow.

Throwing caution to the winds every night, so as not to be seen, Bhogi, along with Santok and either Mangal or

Ranchhod, went to the tree and chopped leaves to feed to the buffaloes. Despite the ghastly location and the ghoulish echoes the wind created as it rustled the leaves of the banyan tree, Bhogi worked on. After the talk he had had with the old man in Ahmedabad, he no longer feared superstition and knew that God would always protect and help those who helped themselves. By undertaking such a measure he was definitely helping himself, and God would never allow anything to harm him.

In addition, one by one they cut small branches into tiny pieces, ground them in a mortar, mixed them with milk and swallowed the thick paste themselves, thus obtaining essential nutrients. In this way the family managed to survive along with their priceless buffaloes. Even the buffaloes had become sensitive to human needs: they started eating less, yet gave more milk.

When Bhogi was three years old, an astrologer had predicted that he would suffer three incidents which had the potential to kill him, but he would escape all three. The first of the three happened on one of those summer nights in the samshan itself.

Bhogi was chopping branches off the banyan tree one night, while his aunt stood below. To be safe he always sat on the solid end of the branch so that when the branch fell, he wouldn't go down with it. It was taking longer than usual and his aunt called from below, telling him to come down for dinner. He said he'd be down as soon as he was finished, not relishing the prospect of having to trek back again after dinner. His aunt responded by threatening him with two tight slaps if he did not come down immediately. Dejected and a little angry, he climbed down from the tree. The moment he came down, the branch he was cutting suddenly splintered and fell off the trunk. Had Bhogi still been there, he would have fallen from a height of 20ft and suffered multiple broken bones.

A week after this incident, late but heavy rain showers ended one of the worst summers in the history of the region. Bhogi went back to Ahmedabad and life went on as usual.

9

Out of the Woods

'Life consists not in holding good cards but in playing those you hold well.' – Josh Billings

The exam students take after the eleventh grade is one that determines their career path and entire future. Consequently, students spend every waking hour studying for it. While it was a little easier back in Bhogi's era than it is today, they also had fewer resources then. He had no problems studying in Ahmedabad, where the city provided electricity for its residents. Back home during the summer, however, was a different issue. So again, Bhogi came up with a solution. He studied underneath the gas-powered street lamps every night, diligently turning pages and making notes as the moon rose and the crickets chirped, and working with machine-like efficiency to ensure that he did well.

The principal of C.N. High School was a renowned poet named Sneharashmi. He had announced a poetry competition for the graduating class, with a promise of a full scholarship for college education of the outgoing student . Bhogi wrote a poem on a topic he was intimately familiar with: death. All he had to do was to recall the memories of his parents' deaths and the words automatically flowed. Sneharashmi himself was one of the judges. The results were announced. Bhogi was awarded the first prize, and so was the possibility of a full scholarship for liberal art studies.

Sneharashmi called Bhogi to his office. 'Listen Bhogi,' he began, 'I have never seen you reading literature or speaking up in class about it. I never thought you were interested in liberal arts. How then did you write such a heartrending poem?'

Instead of answering, Bhogi had tears in his eyes. The principal thought that they were the result of his compliment. He continued, 'Bhogi, I know a famous liberal arts college in Delhi. I want you to go there, continue your college studies and shine like I did. Make Gujarat proud of you. You are gifted and I will do anything and everything to make you a successful writer.'

Bhogi was unable to say anything. Finally, tired of his silence, the principal asked in irritation, 'You did not like what I just said?'

Bhogi broke down in tears. 'It is not you, Sir!' he said between sobs. 'My whole life has been a tragic poem. I would very much like to write and speak about what my life has been. Yes, I'm sure it would be healing and therapeutic for me, and may make me famous. However, I have made a promise to myself to become an engineer. I would not have had to make this difficult choice if my mother Kashi hadn't died due to the lack of paved roads in the villages outside the city. She would have proudly wanted me to become a poet. But the suffering that I saw during the horrific drought made me promise myself that I will become a civil engineer and build roads and water reservoirs so that people in small villages do not suffer any more.'

He continued sobbing for several minutes. The principal was moved, but it was hard to console someone who had suffered so much. 'You have my blessings wherever you go, Son. I know you will succeed in reducing the suffering of humanity. My heart goes out to you.'

What followed was Bhogi's determination to qualify for engineering college. The countless hours and endless preparations paid off, as he ended up scoring in the top tier of his class that year. He had the tenth-highest score in Ahmedabad and had the choice of joining any field he wanted, be it medicine, engineering or even the civil service. He chose engineering.

The next few years went by in an absolute blur as Bhogi studied and laboured his way through engineering college. In 1956, he graduated with a degree in civil engineering from the foremost college in Ahmedabad (in those days, fees for higher education were nominal and any qualified person could afford them). He wished to begin his career as an engineer for the Government of India.

Government positions at the time were full, so Bhogi had to wait for an existing engineer at the associate level to either quit his job or be promoted. In the meantime, he took up a job as an assistant lecturer at the university from where he had just graduated. However, the monotony and, indeed, the benefits of a bachelor's existence soon came to an end for Bhogi.

In those days, a marriage that had not been arranged was regarded as highly unconventional and was looked down upon. In 1957, a mere five months after becoming an engineer, news spread fast in the Kadva Patidar community that an eligible bachelor was available. One of Ranchhod's close friends, Shantilal (no relation to the village money lender), came to their house with his cousin. He claimed that he wanted to ask for Bhogi's help on something in the engineering field.

'Bhogi, I am building a house near Vadaj. We have a contractor who we believe is not honest and is stealing cement from us. Would you be able to come with us and tell us if he is cheating us?' Shantilal requested.

'Sure,' Bhogi replied. 'When do you want me to visit your building site? I'm positive that I'll be able to tell you how much cement you would need.'

'I will let you know,' said Shantilal. 'By the way, what are your long-term plans? Do you plan to continue working for the government or start your own business?'

'Well, I don't know yet. I do want to work with the district authorities of Ahmedabad at least for the next ten to fifteen years, as I want to make sure that small villages like Detroj and Dangarva have proper asphalt roads and drinking water.' Bhogi did not go into details as to why he was still fixated on building roads and water reservoirs in the rural areas.

'Would you like a beedi?' Shantilal asked.

'No, thanks. I don't enjoy smoking,' Bhogi politely refused.

'Being in the city, surely you must drink quite a bit?'

Bhogi laughed and said, 'I'm not sure why villagers have these misconceptions about city dwellers. I don't drink either.'

Instead of enquiring about cement or his new house, Shantilal kept asking Bhogi about his personal life. Somewhat bemused, Bhogi wasn't quite sure what Shantilal was up to but he answered the questions anyway.

As it transpired, Shantilal had a niece who was eighteen and was considered by her family to be ready for marriage. Shantilal had come to enquire about Bhogi and check on his character. As a young man with no vices, Bhogi had passed the test with flying colours.

Shantilal soon forwarded an official offer for an arranged marriage to Ranchhod, who was looked upon as the patriarch of the family.

An engineer groom was highly desirable in that era and, indeed, he was the pride of the family. Earlier three proposals had already been turned down since Bhogi was studying in university at the time. Now that he had graduated, however, he had become one of the most eligible bachelors available.

The family that had sent the proposal was of comparable lineage and from the Kadva Patel clan, the same as Bhogi's family. The girl's name was Premila Patel and was a good match in all regards. Their horoscopes were compared and found to complement each other very well.

Shantilal invited Ranchhod and Bhogi to his sister's house for a meeting with Premila. Bhogi had never met a girl with the purpose of marriage before. It seemed that the arrangement had already been finalized, and the meeting was more of a formality than an actual exercise of choice.

Premila came in, bearing a tray with cups of tea, sweets and savouries. She sat next to her mother and looked down. Her head was covered, so that her face was barely visible through the sari.

'How are you?' Bhogi asked.

'I am fine. How are you?' Premila replied with a blush on her face.

'Do you like villages?' Bhogi awkwardly asked, wanting to ascertain her opinion of villagers. Premila looked at her uncle Shantilal, seeking his approval for an answer.

'Oh, you would never have to live in a village once you are an engineer. Isn't that right, Bhogi?' he interjected to avoid any inconvenient answers.

They all drank their tea. Shantilal then lit his beedi and offered one to Bhogi, who again reminded him that he neither smoked nor ever intended to.

The whole meeting lasted about thirty minutes. Bhogi went home with Ranchhod. His cousin asked if he approved of the girl. Bhogi wasn't quite sure what to say, as this was the first time he had met the girl. Based on those thirty minutes, he hesitantly nodded in agreement. On the girl's side, Premila had very little or no say. Shantilal and her father had already decided that Bhogi was the best possible match they could hope to find, and they conveyed their decision to Premila before speaking to Ranchhod. When he communicated both his own and Bhogi's assent, they began preparing for the ceremony. While India had already progressed a great deal from the days of burning widows on the funeral pyres of their deceased husbands, marriage was still a very strict and a controlled tradition. To formalize the affair, the girl's parents sent a silver rupee coin and a coconut as a token of their promise to marry their daughter to Bhogi. Traditionally the coin and coconut, which in essence show an unbreakable commitment, were sent to the groom's parents. At the time of marriage, the groom's mother brought the coin and coconut back and exchanged them for the bride at the ceremony. Since Bhogi's parents weren't alive, the token was sent to Ranchhod instead and Santok played the role of the mother. When the rupee is sent, the marriage is given the final go-ahead. While Bhogi had the option to refuse an arranged marriage, and demand the right to meet the girl before agreeing, women were not accorded the same privilege. If the parents had decided, the matter had entered the plane of non-negotiability and the only way to escape the commitment would be elopement, which was actually an occasional practice. Divorces were absolutely out of the question. Indeed, girls sometimes came home to their parents bruised and crying from the wrath of a drunken husband, only to have the parents send them right back.

Fortunately, Bhogi didn't drink and was a good person as Premila confirmed during their brief courtship, during which he was allowed to speak with her while chaperoned. Bhogi too was convinced that marrying Premila wasn't a bad decision.

The wedding started off with a bang. Organized by the bride's family the ceremony was held in the village, and what a grand event it was. An enormous coloured tent was erected, within which 300 guests were offered a feast. Sweets were given to all, and those left over were kept aside to give to the poor. As if the food wasn't enough, the continuous sharp and rhythmic drumbeats of the dholi ensured that no one remained away from the celebratory mood. Old men set the pace by dancing with great vigour alongside younger people who eagerly matched their feverish pace. Everyone, especially the women, was dressed in their finest clothes as the wedding of one individual was often the ground at which another marriage was often decided upon.

Finally, the wedding rites were performed. As Bhogi's

parents weren't alive to fulfil their role in the ritual, their spots were taken by Ranchhod and his wife. The Brahmin priest uttered lines of ancient Sanskrit texts and blessed the marriage with many mantras, wishing luck and stability to the newlywed couple. The ceremony revolved around a holy fire lit in a makeshift fireplace with offerings of fruit, grain flowers and ghee. Both Bhogi and Premila had to walk around the holy fire seven times, with Bhogi leading Premila. After completing each circle, they had to take a vow or holy commandment to do everything possible to help and live for each other. The seven rounds of the fire signified their commitment to each other not only for the duration of their life, but for the next six as well.

That evening everyone was in the mood for celebration, except for Bhogi. He liked his new bride and in-laws. He had no complaints or displeasure about anything. But something was still missing: his mother. Tears had appeared at the corners of his eyes while he was taking his marriage vows with Premila. If only Kashi could have lived to see this day, if only she could have carried the coconut and the coin at the head of the groom's entourage, if only she could have seen her son proudly marrying a respectable girl . . . how happy she would have been.

Eventually, the festivities came to an end and Bhogi returned to Ahmedabad with his wife. As if God Himself had decided to give Bhogi a wedding gift, a mere week after the wedding an associate engineer working for the state of Gujarat was promoted, which allowed Bhogi to take his position and commence the work that became his life's passion: civil engineering and construction.

The concept of an arranged marriage is still largely unfathomable to many in Western society. Indeed, it is hard to understand how one can devote their entire life to someone they couldn't possibly have loved considering that they had barely met each other before getting married. However, the attitude of someone getting into an arranged marriage was usually different. From childhood Bhogi had been taught that love would grow once a couple was married, and he believed it wholeheartedly.

10

Gathering Clouds

'The superstition of science scoffs at the superstition of faith.' – James Froude

During Bhogi's tenure as an associate engineer, Premila became pregnant with their first child. After seventeen hours of gruelling labour, Jatin Bhogi Patel came into this world. The apple of his parents' eyes, he was given the best education possible from the beginning. Jatin would eventually grow up to follow in his father's footsteps as an engineer, but with the help of money, the best schools and, most importantly, with both his parents. In other words, without any of the hardships his father had to go through.

Jatin's birth proved to be particularly troublesome. To begin with, it happened while Bhogi had a major confrontation with his superior officer and his job was in the line of fire. Already stressed and frustrated about his career and his future, the vast demands that a newborn child brings with it only doubled the pressure on him and his family. While Bhogi himself was able to deal with it, Premila was a different story.

She woke up screaming on the fifth night after Jatin's birth and gesticulated wildly, pointing outside. 'Bhogi, help me!' she yelled. 'They are here to take my son away. Look at them, outside in the shadows.'

Often having to work in hostile areas, Bhogi had been given an Enfield rifle for protection that he kept locked in his bedroom cabinet when he wasn't out on the job. He awoke with a jolt and after hearing Premila insist that there were men outside, he ran for the gun. Kidnappings for ransom weren't unheard of then. Bhogi decided to teach them a lesson.

'Stay here; don't leave this room,' he warned Premila. 'I'll go and deal with them. They think they can kidnap my son from me?'

Bhogi couldn't see anyone from the window, and assumed they had hidden themselves. He calmly walked downstairs with the gun raised. He didn't make a single sound until he opened the door and barged outside, yelling, 'Come out, you bastards!'

There was no one.

Bhogi thought that Premila must have had a nightmare and came back upstairs. But despite his insistence that there was no one on the premises, she insisted that they were still there. 'Look in the shadows; they're lurking with their dark hoods. Keep them away; they will kill my son,' she continued to cry out loud. 'They've been following us since when we passed Dudheshwar on our way back from the hospital.'

Bhogi was mystified and a little annoyed. 'Oh stop fussing,' he said. 'You had a nightmare. Now go back to sleep.'

Premila insisted that she wasn't dreaming. The ruckus awakened Bhailal and he came into the room. 'What's wrong, Bhogi? Why are all of you awake?' he said while rubbing his eyes.

'Premila keeps saying that some hooded men followed us from Dudheshwar and that they're trying to take Jatin away. Nonsense.'

'I'm telling you, they will take my son away to Dudheshwar and kill him! I see six of them, and they are speaking in Arabic,' Premila continued hysterically.

'Did you by any chance pass by that kabrastan near Dudheshwar?' Bhailal asked.

'We did, on our way from the hospital. I also remember talking to my friend who had got on the bus from Dudheshwar and asked him to come with us for a cup of tea,' Bhogi replied.

'Did you say "chalo"?' Bhailal asked.

'Obviously. How else are you supposed to ask someone to come with you?' Bhogi snapped. He knew quite well what Bhailal was getting at.

'There you go! You should have never uttered that word near a cemetery! I'm sure that ghosts hovering around found their way to you when you said it. Do you realize how hard it will be to get rid of these demonic entities? They may even manage to kill the poor child,' Bhailal said.

'Oh, both of you are completely wrapped up in this nonsense. You know, I used to go into a samshan every night during the drought and cut leaves from the tree for the buffaloes to eat?'

Even as Bhogi maintained a brave front, doubts were swimming in his mind. He remembered those lonely nights when he had to travel to the most inaccessible locations in Gujarat, and remembered seeing and hearing things that no man could explain. He remembered when they were repairing a bridge in Gir, he stumbled across an altar sticky with fresh blood. What was it that the workmen had said?

'Sahib, in the jungles there are things that will make your skin crawl. Noises that come out of the air. People who walk and yet leave no tracks or traces behind. Men that turn into beasts. Ladies that wander eerily in the moonlight. We have seen lions and leopards hiding and cowering in fright from the evils that lurk in the dark places of our world.'

With a sudden shiver, Bhogi remembered what another had added.

'Sahib, it is said that black witches live in these forests. The nawab once did a royal hunt right around here, some fifty years ago. His mightiest knight, Agnivesh, was pursuing a lion and got separated from the rest of the company. He didn't return at night. They found his once spirited horse crouched in fear the next morning with an empty saddle. A few hours later, they found Agnivesh. He was curled in a ball, his armour and sword cast aside. All he said was, "The hooded men are here. They are watching from the shadows. The hooded men are here."'

Suddenly, Bhogi was seeing the workmen's stories unfolding in real life. He had to get help.

No expenses were spared in trying to solve the problem. Priest after priest was brought to the household to rid the evil spectres, although none but Premila had seen or experienced their presence. The rooms were blessed countless times, and gallons of holy water were sprayed over the floors and walls, and Premila herself during the next two years. And yet, her state remained unchanged. The visions appeared and she still felt the evil eye gazing upon her with undisguised fury. The hooded men were still stalking her wherever she went, always watching and waiting for her to slip.

Convinced that the entity was stronger than could be driven out by regular priests, the family began to take more drastic steps. Bhailal took Premila to see a specialist in ghost removal and exorcisms of evil at the Sarangpur Mandir located 100km away. Unlike previous journeys around the state, this one was much easier now that Bhogi was a state engineer and had access to government transport. Bhailal and Bhogi's driver took Premila to the legendary temple to finally remove the demons that were assailing her.

Sarangpur Mandir is a temple devoted to Hanuman Dada, the Vanar Lord. Hanuman took the form of an enormous ape, and was a devotee of Lord Rama. Years ago his tale was told in the Ramayana, in which Rama routed the devils and demons of the world in a climactic battle with Hanuman as his premier general. Hanuman was specially noted for his war upon the rakshasas and the demons of Lanka, and was seen as the foremost protector of mankind against the evils of the spirit world. His name alone inspired fear amongst the incarnations of malevolence, as it brought forth memories of the havoc his mace wrought amongst their ranks during the Great War. For this reason, any ritual involving ridding the presence of an evil entity was conducted in the name of Hanuman.

Sarangpur was in a fearsome location. Electricity still hadn't reached the temple at the time, and it was literally one of the darkest places on earth. The temple was situated in the middle of nowhere and was surrounded by wild jungles, filled with leopards, panthers and Asiatic lions. Tales of children wandering into the bowels of the forest and never being seen again were a favourite of the old wives of the region, and usually ended in a gruesome manner to give warning of the dangers of wilful behaviour. The graveyard rule still applied and no one was allowed to utter the fateful word 'chalo' in the small village surrounding the temple, because the indiscriminate command was a cue for ghosts to follow.

The temple's fame rose because it was the site of a miracle when it was first constructed in the eighteenth century. As it was being dedicated Hanuman Himself was said to have entered the idol and the idol's head came alive, moving from side to side until finally fixing itself in a new position. People suffering from 'supernatural' ailments, from across India, came to the temple to be rid of pursuing ghosts. All day, priests who had devoted their lives to Hanuman bhakti conducted rituals, without any fees, to rid individuals of spirits.

It was there that Bhailal took Premila. The priest there performed a long and arduous ceremony to rid her of the demons that plagued her. To begin with, he sprayed her head with holy water and placed an orange mark of kanku on her forehead. Then he chanted prayers and mantras long forgotten by most of mankind. He touched her head with a red-hot iron rod, making her shriek with pain. Next, he repeatedly pressed heated coals to her chin to provoke the ghosts into exiting the body. The process lasted for over an hour and the only result was a series of burn marks on Premila's face.

The priest told them that the problem was more deep-rooted than he had imagined and that Premila would be looked at by the high priest of the mandir the next morning. After a careful examination and a detailed reading of her horoscope, the high priest thought that he had found the root of the problem. He diagnosed that Premila had been suffering from a spirit possession and a haunting that had been caused by a distant relative jealous of her family's success. That relative, who was named by the psychic, had visited a black magician and had paid a handsome amount of money to place her under demonic possession. The spirits were merely waiting for an invitation and, when Bhogi had uttered the fateful word next to the cemetery, had come to haunt her. The high priest asserted that he could cure her, but Bhailal would first have to undergo a frightening ritual himself. He insisted that Bhogi himself not be allowed to conduct the ceremony; the scriptures held that if someone too close to Premila conducted it, the demons would take advantage of their emotional connection and merely move to haunt him instead.

The cure was almost as terrifying as the diagnosis itself. Bhailal would have to enter a samshan at midnight two days later on Kali Chaudas, the Evil Fourteenth, said to be the most evil night of the Hindu calendar. On that night, all the dark spirits of the world were said to emerge and black magic was at its strongest for the entire duration of the night. Bhailal would have to challenge the spirits on the night they were at their zenith. He would have to burn incense in the grove underneath a banyan tree growing there, and sit until midnight. Then, throw a coconut hard on the ground and smash it to bits. Following that, toss grains in front and behind himself, all the while chanting the *Hanuman Chalisa*, summoning his family's guardian spirits to fight off the evil spirits plaguing Premila. Finally, he was to sprinkle a pinch of salt over his left shoulder, signifying the end of the ritual and allowing the spirits to rest.

The growls of wild animals filled the air as Bhailal entered the samshan. Kali Chaudas was a dark and cloudy night, and not even the soft white glow of moonlight illuminated his way. The little light he had was from a flickering wax candle, whose flame kept getting blown out by the fierce wind. He sat on the ground as the bloodcurdling cry of a wolf floated through the darkness, accompanied by the howls of wild dogs that seemed to be harassing it. Paying no attention to the frightening surroundings or the legends of the ghouls that emerged from samshans on that night, Bhailal went to work. He sat on the ground underneath the banyan tree and improvised a prayer area, chanting the verses the priest had specified while placing images of gods and goddesses on a small rug he had brought along. He lit three sticks of sandalwood incense in accordance with the priest's instructions. The sweet scent mixed with the lingering smoke of the crematorium, lightening his mind and softening his awareness. Shaking his head clear, he began to recite the *Hanuman Chalisa*, praising and calling upon Lord Hanuman for help and deliverance from the evil spirits afflicting his sister-in-law.

Suddenly, a bolt of lightning lit the samshan in a ghostly glow and the resounding crack of thunder made Bhailal jump. He calmed down and completed the first recitation of the *Hanuman Chalisa*. Suddenly, a branch that had been swaying ever since he began broke from above and nearly hit his head. Shaken, he took to his heels and almost fled the premises before regaining his composure and trudging back to the sinister tree and the rug and prayer circle he had created under it, lighting up another stick of incense.

The rest of the night passed without any incident, and Bhailal returned home.

After the completion of this complex ritual, Premila was taken to the Sarangpur priest. He exorcised her again and she was deemed to have been cured. For the next six months, she was forbidden from eating anything oily or sweet.

After listening to this story, Maharshi interrupted Bhogi.

While the tale of demonic possession and jealousy-inspired black magic made an excellent story, it was nothing beyond that according to Maharshi. He told Bhogi that in today's society, depression and the subsequent mental illness could just as easily have been attributed to the rare condition of post-partum psychosis following pregnancy. Women who suffer from it undergo enormous weight-loss, sleep periods lasting for more than forty-eight hours, or even hallucinations and severe delusions. This was the very same disease that affected Andrea Yates and Melanie Stokes back in America, he asserted. But back then, the unexplained was always attributed to the realm of the abstract and the religious. In a fit of bravado, Maharshi even proclaimed that he would specifically request that his wedding be held on Kali Chaudas to prove that it was nonsense.

In response, Bhogi gave him a sly smile.

'Tell me,' he began, 'what happened to this Andrea Yates and Melanie Stokes?'

'Well, Yates drowned her five children in a bathtub and Stokes killed herself.'

'So, there you have it. You argue that the science of your Western world was better than the rituals we undertook and yet, the women your hospitals diagnosed ended up killing either themselves or others. All the while, with the help of her faith, Premila recovered and became completely healthy. Even if the haunting was a figment of her mind, is the end result not all that matters?'

Maharshi really didn't have a response to that, since Premila had recovered. Whether it was the complex ritual bravely undertaken by Bhailal on Kali Chaudas, the effects of the priest's diet regimen or perhaps her inner strength that cured Premila of the illness, one will never know. However, what matters was that she was healthy once more and, following the cure, became pregnant with Kashyap Bhogi Patel.

11

Lightning Strikes

'No experience is a cause of success or failure. We do not suffer from the shock of our experiences so-called trauma – but we make out of them just what suits our purposes.' – Alfred Adler

Life was moving at a faster pace for his family than Bhogi could have imagined. On 1 October 1961, a day before Mahatma Gandhi's birthday, Premila gave birth to Kashyap. When he was still a newborn and Jatin was a toddler Bhogilal suffered the second of the three predicted accidents, one that brought him inches away from death's door and the chariot of Yamaraj, the God of Death.

Since Bhogilal, Bhailal and Ranchhod all lived together, they shared a common bathroom. The geyser they used was not a very advanced one: two electric probes had to be put into water, after which the switch was turned on and the water would heat. Then, before touching the water, the switch was turned off and the probes removed, leaving a bucket full of hot water to be used at leisure.

One morning Bhogi called out to his wife, 'I'm about to bathe. Is the geyser off?'

'Yes, I turned it off after bathing Jatin,' Premila answered.

'OK, I'm going to go take a bath then.'

Bhogi entered the bathroom, undressed and grabbed a bar of soap. Unknown to him or to anybody else in the house, the geyser had broken after Premila used it. Despite the switch having been turned off, electricity was still flowing through the water when Bhogi touched it.

The next thing Bhogi knew – he woke up in the dirty bed of a hospital three days later, with Bhailal and Jatin at his bedside. He could only muster the strength to ask one question: 'What happened?'

Bhailal told him that as soon as his hands had touched the water, he got a severe shock. Premila and Bhailal heard his screams and ran to the bathroom. Knowing that touching his body would simply cause him to be electrocuted along with Bhogi, Bhailal had pulled the geyser's power plug out of its socket. The current had instantly stopped, but Bhogi fell down. Bhailal watched almost in slow motion as Bhogi swayed and fell headfirst onto the concrete floor, cracking his skull. He lay on the floor, unconscious and immobile. Premila watched as Bhailal turned him over. When she saw her husband's bloody face, she turned and vomited. Bhogi's blood quickly spread on the ground, mixing with the spilled water and coating the floor in a sickening shade of red. Bhailal ran outside, hailed a taxi and took him to the hospital.

Those were the days long before CAT scans and MRIs were invented. The doctors only knew that Bhogilal's fall had added a cracked skull to the troubles caused by the electricity.

They drew their conclusions from this fact. The fractured skull meant head trauma that could have been severe enough to induce a brain haemorrhage. The chance of recovering from such a severe injury was small. The extent of damage was still a complete mystery to them. Only time would tell how badly the incident had actually affected Bhogi. They were frank with Bhailal. 'We don't know for sure, but it looks like his injuries could be very severe.'

'How severe?'

'Well, he is currently in a coma. To be honest with you, he has about a 15 per cent chance of waking up from his coma. And then, he has an even smaller chance of waking up without permanent brain damage. We're afraid that chances are he'll be mentally handicapped. For all we know, he could wake up in a vegetable state, or perhaps mentally retarded. There is no telling what kind of damage has occurred.'

'What is the chance that he'll be mentally incapacitated?'

'There is no way to tell for certain. We don't know what his brain has gone through, but the chance that he'll be completely normal is near-zero.'

For the next few days, while Bhogi stayed in a constant state of unconsciousness, his family could only wait and pray by his bedside, unsure if Bhogi would ever wake up and if he did, what state his mind would be in.

After four distressing days and nights passed, Bhogi finally awoke. Bhailal started weeping when he heard Bhogi speak, and the glint in his eyes told Bhailal that Bhogi had somehow managed to defeat the expectations of the doctors and come back to normalcy.

The doctors said that even one more second of exposure to the electricity would have guaranteed that Bhogi had no chance of recovery. To make matters worse, his brain had been endangered twice: first by the severe electric shock he had suffered, and second by the subsequent fall and the fractured skull. He was already more than lucky to have managed to wake up from the coma unharmed. The added bonus that he still retained control over his body and his sanity marked his recovery as nothing short of a miracle.

Another year later Premila became pregnant again and, after a normal delivery, gave birth to their first daughter, Trupti Bhogi Patel.

Bhogi's life began to become more and more disconnected from the rest of his extended family. The frequent fights between the wives and children of his family soon led them to split households. Being the highest earner of his family, Bhogi decided to build his own house.

The new house was constructed in the-then newly developed neighbourhood of Maneklal Park. It had two floors and sat on a third of an acre of land, which was quite a lot for any house in Ahmedabad. It was solidly built and boasted four bedrooms, although the family slept in two. In other words, it was enough to house the children even after marriage, which was Bhogi's original intention. Bhailal moved in for a few years.

The years in the new house began to pass, and life settled into a routine. Kashyap turned eight and was showing a healthy interest in school. In 1969, however, things changed.

Kashyap came back from school one day with a very high fever and vomiting. 'Did you eat something from the hawker? I told you not to eat or drink from those streetside vendors near your school,' Premila scolded him.

'No Mother, I did not eat anything at school. My stomach is hurting and my body is burning all over.' Kashyap had a difficult time even articulating his complaints.

That night, his condition worsened. He became delirious. He woke up several times at night and began speaking incomprehensible words. Morning arrived, and Bhogi hadn't slept a wink. Kashyap's entire body had turned yellow.

The family doctor was summoned. He diagnosed Kashyap with a severe case of jaundice. Superstition still held sway in the Patel household. Again, Premila's gullible nature chose to supplement medicinal remedies with more religious ones. Kashyap was sent to see a traditional healer who claimed that he would be able to cure the jaundice by merely whispering a few chants while spraying his head with water. In the meanwhile, Kashyap started taking the antibiotics prescribed to him by the doctor.

The healer lived in the oldest part of Ahmedabad, within the inner city walls made by the Mughal emperors. He stayed in an area known as Dariapur, where Premila's sister Vidya also happened to live. Kashyap was sent to stay with her. He was allowed to eat only chickpeas for the entire duration of the black magic ritual. The neighbourhood was renowned as a place where Hindus and Muslims had lived side by side for centuries in peace and happiness.

12

Apocalypse

'For our cause I too am prepared to die, but for no cause, my friend, will I be prepared to kill.' – Mahatma Gandhi

Ahmedabad experienced some of the worst religious riots in the twentieth century. The neighbours who had lived side by side for centuries, dating back to almost 200 to 300 years, had suddenly started looking at each other with suspicion and hatred thanks to the British imperialist policies of divide and conquer to rule the colonies. This philosophy was so successful that even post-independence, Indian rulers had elected to maintain and nurture this mutual hatred for sustaining their selfish rules.

The British had always used the divide and rule strategy. To bolster the strength of their regime, they ensured that the local population remained distrustful of each other so as to prevent the unity that leads to rebellion. Seeds of doubt about the safety of Muslims in an independent India with a Hindu majority were subtly sown.

However, the British had no idea of the awful power of what they had unleashed. What had begun as a way to maintain order grew far beyond the ability of the British to control, as the seeds of mistrust bloomed into threats of violence that eventually led to the partition of India into three pieces: India, East Pakistan and West Pakistan. The British were forced to watch in horror as millions of innocent civilians were ruthlessly slaughtered by their own countrymen, and communities that had lived in peace for hundreds of years took up arms against one another.

Although Gujarat was not affected too much by the post-Independence riots, Pakistani spies had been caught among the Muslim population of Gujarat in the early Sixties. The war in 1965 with Pakistan, against which Gujarat was the first line of defence, had already created a suspicious attitude towards Muslims. The much-beloved chief minister of Gujarat, Balwantrai Mehta, had lost his life when his plane was shot down as he was trying to visit troops on the front. His death had pushed the entire state into mourning, soon accompanied by anger; this only increased the communal divide, as Pakistan was an Islamic republic. Events had been building up for the past four years, and communal anger was already smouldering. Shambuji Maharaj, a popular religious leader, was pushing for a nationwide ban on cow slaughter and chose to base his efforts in Ahmedabad. His sermons often included condemnation of the 'vile' and 'barbarous' nature of Muslim slaughterhouses, as tradition dictated that animals eaten by Muslims be slain in the halal manner which involved the slicing the throat of the animal and bleeding it to death. Hindu nationalists became particularly active, setting up pro-Hindu camps across the state. The powder keg was being laid since the last four years. All it needed now was a match.

That match was lit at 3.45 p.m. on 18 September. A small fair was taking place in Ahmedabad. The festival was a minor religious one, attended by only a small gathering of the most devout sadhus. A herd of cattle was being driven along the road where the festival was being held. Their destination was the slaughterhouse, and the herder was a Muslim. A heated argument broke out, and it lit the powder keg. The fight between the sadhus and the herder quickly escalated until, in a fit of rage, the herder struck a sadhu in the head with a metal stick, splitting open his skull. Suddenly, all of Ahmedabad rose up in arms.

Troublemakers, delighted at this turn of events, quickly distributed machetes and similar weapons to Hindu mobs and set themselves at the head of the mobs, chanting slogans and inciting them further. The Muslim side was far from inactive and almost every mosque's loudspeaker rang with a call to arms, inciting the substantial minority to brutally murder any Hindu to be found – whether an armed rioter or an innocent baby.

By nightfall, the city was ablaze and the riots showed no sign of stopping. The police were powerless before the sheer number of the mobs; and some policemen actively joined them. The politicians were unwilling to intervene; some abetted the rioters out of the desire of improving their vote banks and appealing to the nationalist trend that had seized the state.

Bhogi was on service duty that evening. He had been busy with the construction of a road on the outskirts of the city, and so didn't have a chance to return home that evening. He didn't realize what was happening. The government had given him a jeep and a driver. As his work often took him to dangerous areas inhabited by dacoits, they also appointed an armed police constable to accompany him. It was the three of them, out on a lonely road, surveying the land for the building of a bridge that had collapsed further down.

They saw abnormal lights, with an orange haze, were popping up all around the city. They tried the radio for information, but the transmission equipment in the jeep wasn't working. Bhogi knew by instinct that despite the lack of communication, the powder keg had finally been lit. He had not been blind to the growing religious tensions that had been tugging at every corner of Ahmedabad for the past few months, and he feared something like that had happened.

Bhogi's first thought was about his family and their safety. Yet, he felt secure as he was aware that they had a rifle and Bhailal was at home with them. Precious few firearms were available in the state of Gujarat and a real gun would scare the daylights out of any approaching crowd. They lived in a neighbourhood that was overwhelmingly Hindu anyway; no Muslim mob would have the guts to make its way there. After a moment's doubt, Bhogi felt reassured that his family would be safe amid the strength of their neighbours and Bhailal wielding his rifle.

Bhogi decided that it was his responsibility as a civil servant to help maintain law and order in the area and, if possible, help coordinate rescue operations, investigate the matter and try to provide first-aid attention to those who needed it.

Bhogi's driver, who had been his companion for the past few years, immediately and fearlessly turned the jeep back towards the city. Bhogi glanced at the constable. The young police officer was thoughtfully stroking his moustache with his left hand while lightly gripping his Enfield rifle with the other. Bhogi knew by his tacit calmness that he could count on the man should the situation turn ugly. They sat silently as the city came into view, and found that it was much worse than any of them had imagined.

The city was burning. The electricity had gone but everything was visible in the reddish glare of the flames that were springing up, right, left and centre. It seemed that hell had been unleashed on Ahmedabad in all of its fury. The screams of innocent victims were drowned out by yells of 'Allah-u-Akbar' and its answering Hindu call 'Har Har Mahadev!'

Even as they drove in, a woman, no older than twenty-five, her face streaked with blood, ran up to the jeep. She had recognized the insignia of the government of Gujarat and saw it as her last hope. She had a bundle in her hands.

'Please Sahib, please,' she begged. 'Save me and my child, Sahib! They are coming after us. They have machetes and sticks, and they have already cut my husband into pieces. They want me now. Please Sahib, you are our only hope.'

With a jolt Bhogi realized that the bundle the woman was carrying was a little baby. 'Don't worry. Get in,' he said. He placed his hand reassuringly on her back and added, 'Don't be scared. You will be all right.'

Bhogi then asked his stoic constable to pass him a revolver. It was right then that a marching mob suddenly burst on to the scene. He could tell from the red chandlas they had drawn on their heads that they were Hindus, and that they had come for the poor woman quivering in the back of his jeep, shielding her baby in her arms.

The leader, wearing an orange shirt and khaki shorts, stood at the head of the mob. There were between twenty to thirty men; Bhogi couldn't be sure. They were carrying torches among many other weapons, ranging from knives to already bloodstained swords. They looked drunk with rage and murderous intent was written all over their faces, gleaming in the flickering flames of the torches they held up.

The leader knew Bhogi was a Hindu by the rudraksh he spotted on Bhogi's wrist, and addressed him as such. 'Sir, we are here for the traitorous Muslim swine in the back of your jeep. Do not fear; you will come to no harm, but we need the girl.'

'Absolutely not! I am a representative of the government of Gujarat. You are in direct violation of its laws. Disband at once.'

This response didn't please the leader. 'It's not a question of laws, Sahib. You are in no position to make demands. See, there are thirty of us and three of you. We are being generous by telling you to go away quietly. Now give us the girl and the bastard of a child with her, or suffer the same fate as her husband! Be a real Hindu!'

With that, the leader raised his lathi high in the air and the crowd behind roared with approval.

At this, Bhogi stood up and fired the revolver in the air. The constable also rose and fired his rifle. They both then took aim at the leader. 'You are a disgrace to Hindu's everywhere. Disband now, or we will shoot you dead where you stand. No one is doing anything to this woman. Go home, you animals!' Bhogi shouted.

As the leader glowered in response, Bhogi fired a warning shot near his feet. With that the attacker realized that this battle was lost, and he went along his way.

Bhogi finally sat down. The poor woman in the back could only whimper her thanks; the chains of fear had rendered her almost mute. He nodded and said, 'They were cowards; not Hindus. There is no bravery in attacking the innocent and no religion can pride itself on spilling the blood of others. What I did was something any decent person would do. Please do not thank me; I was just following my duty and conscience.'

They drove on further until suddenly they reached what appeared to be a battlefield. In front of them was a narrow street with three-storey buildings on either side. Bhogi immediately detected the stench of ganja permeating the surroundings. The neighbourhood was renowned for being lined by Hindu residents on one side and Muslim on the other. As he watched, an almost surreal scene unfolded in front of him. He saw a group of ten Muslims, clearly under the influence of marijuana and armed with cricket bats and wooden sticks, saunter down the road and into the neighbourhood, all the while chanting 'Saale Hindu Murdabad!' He saw Hindus, almost four times in number, all lining the rooftops. The ten who had entered the street apparently hadn't noticed the groups gathering above them and didn't anticipate meeting such a large hostile mob. They were most likely expecting to set upon individual households one by one, pillaging, murdering and possibly worse.

Bhogi silently watched the avid preparations of the Hindus. They had gathered on the terraces, each carrying what seemed to be odd mixtures of petrol and kerosene cans of all sizes, containers of motor oil, a collection of rags and over a hundred glass bottles and corks. This was apparently the 'artillery' for the Hindu side of the fight, and the eclectic collection of goods was actually vital for what happened next.

As Bhogi watched, the bottles were filled with petrol or kerosene and then a little motor oil. Petrol-soaked rags were partially stuffed inside the bottles before they were sealed with corks. The Hindus were making Molotov cocktails.

As Bhogi continued to watch, the first batch of crude bombs was ready. The rags were lit with matches and then hurled towards the Muslim mob marching below and also at the Muslim-owned houses on the other side of the street, which were all well within the throwing range for most of the men on the rooftops. Nine out of ten bombs exploded on impact, spewing burning gasoline in their periphery and burning anything that was in their range, be it wood, stone or human flesh. The motor oil that was added to the mixture made the fire sticky and hard to put out, ensuring the flames continued to burn. There were little children up on the rooftops, eagerly joining in the improvised factory, and cocktails were churned out like butter. The stronger men then ignited and threw, alternating targets between the Muslim mobs below and the apartments on the other side. Fortunately (or unfortunately, depending on whose side one was taking), most houses were made of stone and didn't catch fire or burn down. The streets, however, already littered with countless amounts of flammable junk and waste, ignited only too readily and within an hour the street resembled a scene from the lower pits of hell.

The Muslim side saw the practicality of the 'artillery brigade' and soon tried to start making Molotovs on a roof of their own. Unfortunately, they weren't farsighted enough to choose a roof that was outside the range of the Hindus' cocktails. The moment their actions were sighted, two bombs were hurled onto their roof. The bombs exploded and in turn ignited the many litres of petrol the Muslims had ardently brought up to the roof, spewing an enormous fireball that rapidly rose in the sky and completely demolished the entire building, causing countless casualties. Most of the ten Muslims who had originally set out had been burned alive in the meanwhile; their piteous screams drowned out by the explosions and the yells of the Hindus above.

Sick to his stomach, Bhogi sat down. He had just been witness to the absolute worst of humanity and he could do nothing to save any of the individuals involved. He told his driver to drive them home.

They arrived at the crack of dawn, with the city still sweltering behind them. Bhogi was greatly saddened by the events he had seen. He had tried to follow the footsteps of Gandhi, who forbade any type of violence. He had only witnessed the aftermath of the deaths of his beloved parents and his brother Bhikhu; he had never seen the process of death by killing. At least, he felt, he had abided by the call of duty and humanity by safely escorting a Muslim woman and her child to a relief camp established at the Maleksaban Stadium. He was now worried about the safety of his own son and sister-in-law Vidya who lived in a neighbourhood adjoining a Muslim locality.

He could not help thinking about Gandhi's famous quote: 'An eye for an eye will turn the whole world blind'.

Bhogi, along with Bhailal, rode in his jeep to Padma Pole in the Kalupur area where Vidya lived. Kashyap was staying with her to recover from jaundice. The area happened to be one of the frontlines in the riot. Rumours were floating that the whole city was in flames and hundreds of innocent civilians were murdered and slaughtered like animals under the frenzy of religious extremism.

What Bhogi saw was insurmountable hatred, mistrust and suspicion between the neighbours who had worked shoulder to shoulder during droughts, floods and calamities. Centuries of bonding between generations was wiped out within a matter of seconds, courtesy the divide and rule policy of the British and succeeding politicians. Slowly, during a relatively quiet period, Bhogi took Kashyap and Vidya's family to his new bungalow in the safe area of Naranpura.

Such was not the case in the other areas of Ahmedabad. The riots there went on for the next three days. Such was the inability to stop the violence that the Indian Army was deployed on the streets. It was given shoot-on-sight orders and equipped with automatic weapons, ceasing violence with threats of violence. The screams, gunshots and explosions were replaced with the steady beat of marching battalions of soldiers and the roar of enormous tanks. And then, Ahmedabad lay quiet once again.

The city that emerged from the riots was not the same. The street Vidya and her family lived on now looked like something out of a 1942 Stalingrad. Blood stained the dusty streets a pale-red, some still oozing out of the bodies, leaving them a ghastly white. Flies and other insects feasted on the corpses and vultures from the desert, who normally avoided the city, eagerly flew in, attracted like bees to honey. Rotting corpses became breeding hives for bacteria and viruses, causing the government to issue immediate orders. Internal service officers, in virtual command of districts, ordered each body to be photographed for later identification and then stacked onto a massive pile. When the stacking was complete, a veritable hill formed on the outskirts of the city; it was set aflame that night. The smell of burning flesh hung over the city in the next week, and the smouldering funeral field served to ensure that no one forgot the carnage quickly.

13

The Saga Continues

'Inaction is perhaps the greatest mistake of all.' – Charles Schumer

Bhogi's life was going through a relatively serene period now. After struggling for decades in search of peace and tranquillity, he felt that his life had finally settled into a stable course. He had built a beautiful house in an area inhabited by some of his cousins who, like him, had moved to the big city. His house was big enough to let Bhailal and his family live with him. Old scars of struggles and poverty had slowly disappeared and Bhogi and his family were happy. He had three children: Jatin, Kashyap and Trupti. They studied at the best private school in the state. Bhogi had everything in the world.

His older son, Jatin, had proven to be extremely outspoken from the start. He always displayed a quick temperament, a characteristic that had got him into trouble countless times before. Even when he was a child the family received frequent phone calls from his school, complaining of fights. But, despite this fierce streak, he maintained an affable personality. While his anger could be easily provoked, Jatin was very friendly with those whom he knew and loved. He was also able to maintain his grades very well. The problem was that few could anticipate the sudden changes in his split personality.

Kashyap shared his brother's anger to some extent, but was a relatively calmer individual. His school performances were always ahead of both his siblings.

Trupti, being the youngest of the three and the only girl, was the one who was always indulged and allowed to have her way.

Jatin was the first to complete school. And this was the beginning of the most tragic saga in Bhogi's life. Jatin finished school with good enough grades to pursue any career he wanted, with the exception of medicine. He chose engineering. After another four years of engineering college, he was able to secure a job in the government's pollution board with the role of directing inspections and approving factories for pollution control.

Right around this time his parents thought that since Jatin had reached a level of stability in his life, it was time to look for a bride for him. Following the family tradition, an arranged marriage was the rule. Jatin remembered that one of his cousins had tried to elope and marry a groom of her choice a few years back. The result was the assembly of all the men in the family waiting with lathis and knives for the arrival of the bride and groom. Such was the conservatism in the family.

Premila proudly announced to her friends and neighbours that her son was ready to meet an appropriate girl from a good background and that all matrimonial enquiries were welcome. Bhogi had an excellent reputation in the Patidar clan. As a successful and powerful engineer, he carried an influential position within the government. Girls' parents started lining up with matrimonial proposals. Premila conducted the initial screening of all families, secretly enquired about the girl and her family, and only after two to three stages of vetting, a girl was allowed to speak with Jatin.

After meeting over a dozen prospective brides Jatin decided that he liked Indi, a beautiful young girl from the Patidar clan. Her family owned a cloth business. Premila felt that now she was also in a position to boast about her son's in-laws and their status in society. Indi was kind, pretty and intelligent, and, in all ways, the ideal Indian wife.

One of the biggest problems in Indian marriages – in fact, in most marriages – arises out of the friction between the mother-in-law and daughter-in-law. It is an age-old battle, spanning generations, and incites far too many feuds to be counted. Ironically, while every mother-in-law once had a mother-in-law of her own who constantly argued with her, that never stopped a woman from following in her footsteps. What made it worse was that Premila, like most Indian mothers, insisted that the married couple live with them. Her untreated struggles with depression also changed her personality from the loving kind woman that Bhogi had married, leading to insecure and sometimes irrational paterns of thought. She began to live constant and unwarranted fear of losing Jatin's affection.

Bhogi tried to keep himself above the squabbles, choosing to ignore them, especially as they had become a daily routine.

This strategy didn't help the situation though. What began as typical mother- and daughter-in-law fights soon worsened. Premila, not willing to give up her son, began demanding ridiculous things; for instance, her son and his wife should spend most of their time with her as she was 'scared'. On top of that, Indi was made to continually cook and clean for the entire family. Premila often complained of aches and pains that seemed to have no medical basis, and demanded that her daughter-in-law fulfil her obligations due to her 'inability' to do so herself. 'Ignorance is bliss' seemed to be the mantra around the household for everyone, except Kashyap. Even Jatin merely wanted a life involving both mother and wife equally. Kashyap, however, could not stand what was going on.

Bhogi started feeling overwhelmed by the problems his family was going through. Every single day he came home to arguments, fights and yelling. His wife and daughter-in-law were at war it seemed, and Jatin was doing nothing to remedy the situation. Every evening, exhausted after a long day at work, Bhogi stretched out on his khatlo in the warm sun outside but the peace he longed for was shattered. First his wife came to him and rattled off a long list of complaints about his daughter-in-law. 'She doesn't respect her elders. She doesn't wear decent clothes. She does a shoddy job when she is cleaning. The kitchen has been left a mess. She talks too much. She isn't right. She talks back to me . . . she . . .' And so she went on and on for hours until Bhogi's ears got tired of listening to her.

His daughter-in-law came next, but didn't have the courage to ask him anything beyond whether he would like to have tea. Bhogi gave her a weary smile and say, 'Yes Beti, that would be lovely.'

Then his son came, and Premila berated him for the next few hours as Bhogi tried to distance himself from the scene and get some rest.

Dinner was always an awkward affair, punctuated with snide remarks and headache-inducing arguments. Even Kashyap was drawn into the affair, although on the opposing side.

This went on for months.

One night, as he lay in bed, Bhogi started to think seriously. He had just turned fifty. In the worldly sense, he had already performed the duties of life. One son was a doctor and another was an engineer. He was trying to do a mental tally of his life so far. Was this really what he had left the village for? It almost seemed as if the times when he had no food to eat were far more bearable, because he had a loving family he could go home to. Now, despite his material success, his large house and hefty pay cheque, he was living a life of weariness and discontent.

The next day the routine started as usual. After Bhogi had his cup of tea, the phone rang. Looking for any distraction from his wife's tirade, he went inside and answered the phone.

He immediately wished he hadn't.

It was the police, asking if Bhogi knew Bhailal Patel.

Bhailal's immediate family could not be contacted. His son was in Surat, studying in an engineering college and his other son and daughter were not available. None of them could be reached, so they tried Bhogi.

Bhailal was an athlete and always preferred to walk the 5km to his workplace. He had taken the same route for years. But for the past two days, he had been complaining of a severe ache in his lower back to his wife. Thinking that he was ageing, he didn't bother to do anything about the pain.

As he walked along that fateful morning, Bhailal stopped in front of a local convenience store. He was friendly with almost everyone on that street. He mentioned to someone that his backache had got worse and that standing while teaching that day was going to be very painful. He then left the store, walked a few more feet, and suddenly collapsed.

Someone yelled for a rickshaw. The rickshaw driver immediately took Bhailal to the nearest hospital; the convenience store owner joined him too. The doctor checked Bhailal's pulse. There was none to be found. They pronounced him dead.

Bhailal had had a massive heart attack while walking. He was dead before the rickshaw driver even dragged him in. The people who had taken Bhailal to the hospital knew that he was related to Bhogi Patel. It was one of them who had made the phone call to Bhogi.

Bhogi dropped the receiver. Premila walked in to comment on his carelessness, and then she saw the look of distress on his face. 'Oh my God, Bhogi, what happened? Why are you looking like this?'

'Bhailal . . . dead . . . '

'What! How?'

Bhogi couldn't respond. He sat on the sofa, put his hands on his eyes and started crying softly.

Bhogi didn't speak to anyone for the next few days. He was granted leave from work. The sudden shock put a stop to any arguments in the Patel household. The death affected Bhogi the most. He became totally withdrawn and whatever little interest he had remaining in his family's daily squabbles completely vanished. He was devastated. Bhailal had been in the prime of his health. He jogged for an hour each morning and was more in shape than the students he was teaching. Granted he had a love for fried foods, but he exercised every day.

More painful was the fact that Bhogi couldn't do anything about it. Bhailal had been Bhogi's to protect for so long. Bhogi had foregone so much in order to help raise him when he was a mere twenty-day-old infant. He almost parented him since his father had died. For the entire time they had resided in Ahmedabad, Bhogi had always been there for Bhailal and vice versa. When the riots had struck, it was Bhailal who had defended Bhogi's family. And now, despite all of his efforts, despite all the sacrifices Bhogi had made and everything he had done to try and provide for Bhailal, his brother had been snatched away from him.

Fate had been at its cruellest when it dealt its cards to Bhogi. His older brother, his father, his mother, and now his younger brother – all were dead.

As Bhogi's grief for his brother welled up, it brought forward all those old memories: watching quietly as Bhikhu's body was taken to the crematorium, lighting the pyre of his father with his own hand, the two-day jeep ride to the death of his mother . . . .

The day of the funeral arrived. Bhailal's children had been called back from Surat. They stayed with Bhogi for the next few weeks. As Bhogi watched the Brahmin reciting his verses, he morbidly thought that with his familiarity with Hindu funeral rites, he might as well have conducted the ceremony himself. He watched as Bhailal's body was slowly wrapped in the customary white sheets. He watched as Bhailal's children wept by the side. Bhogi himself couldn't weep any more. All his tears had been used up by the various tragedies that had struck his family.

Bhogi began to question whether he truly had any control over his life at all; and finally concluded that he didn't. He began to realize the truths of life. There wasn't anything he could do to stop fate from taking away his loved ones, and Bhogi now knew it. He had tried to preserve peace in his house; he had tried to provide his family with all the protection possible, but it just wasn't working. He had everything snatched from him: his parents, his brother, his peace, his philosophy.

Bhogi continued watching this erosion in his life. Slowly he started thinking about Lord Krishna and realized that here was this person who had been through much worse situations. Lord Krishna had been destined to witness His entire clan getting destroyed in violence in front of His own eyes, before His own death. *If my dear Lord Krishna had elected to face the death of His own family immediately following the Mahabharata, I have no reason to complain.* Bhogi slowly started bouncing back to life. He remembered an aphorism from the Bhagavad Gita that he had heard every time he was involved in the final rites of his loved ones.

'Jatsya hi Dhruvo Mrutyu, Dhruvam Janma Mrutasya Cha

Tasmadapariharyearthe Na Tvan Shochitumarhasi.'Death is certain for those who are born and rebirth is sure for all those who are deceased. Therefore, you shall not grieve over this inevitable sequence of life and birth.'

While Bhogi entered the mourning period of Bhailal's death, the family conflict resumed its full force. But Bhogi found that he had absolutely no desire to be involved on either side. Life was too important for him to bother with such frivolities.

Right from childhood, Kashyap had an independent streak. He could not stand what was occurring in the household between his mother and sister-in-law. Every night, he protested the mistreatment that was being perpetrated, even though it meant going against his own mother. The split in the family was beginning to show. Instead of Jatin, it was his brother who stood up for his wife. Jatin was simply unable to tell his mother that she was wrong. He threw away his marriage due to his spinelessness. His wife, five months pregnant, finally walked out of the house to return to her parents. Jatin meekly accepted it, but this set into motion an irreversible series of events. Indi, left with no choice, and living in a society that made single motherhood impossible, visited a doctor and had the baby aborted.

Through the entire ordeal even Bhogi didn't raise a voice, busy as he was with trying to cope with his own grief at his brother's passing. He never realized the seriousness of the issue until Premila took the final step. No one but Kashyap spoke up and, when he attempted to interfere, his father warned him to not bother getting involved. This was a major stain on Kashyap's opinion of his father, for whom he had held tremendous respect and regard. Premila, on the other hand, was relieved. She did what she honestly thought was best for the family. Though her intentions were warped, they were made with what she thought would preserve her son's love for her.

A year later Jatin was remarried to Harsha Patel and though he pined for his first wife, he had to make do. The marriage was celebrated without excessive cheer and it seemed that Jatin was living a lie. His new bride didn't have the courage to stand up to Premila and, more importantly, didn't have the money to protest and demand a divorce. So she meekly accepted the ill-treatment meted out to her without a sigh. Throughout the ordeal, Jatin's biggest mistake was taking his mother's side. Unfortunately for him, that mistake continually burned in his mind and he began to get difficult for his mother to control. A spring could only be pushed so far; Jatin would soon reach his breaking point.

Bhogi stopped at this point in the story and sighed. Maharshi knew very well how Jatin's story would end; he was in ninth grade when those events had unfolded and he remembered them quite vividly.

'Beta,' Bhogi said, 'Take this episode to be my biggest mistake of my life. I knew there was wrongdoing in my own house, but I didn't take a stand against it. To this day, I regret it. Had I followed the path of action, had I tried to put a stop to the evil my wife was brewing in my own house, my son would still have been alive today. See your grandfather's example, and understand that Gandhi's words were amongst the truest ever spoken.

'Gandhi warned us that when we ignore the untruth and evil for the sake of expediency, the results are never favourable. Let my mistake teach you this too, Son. What I did was akin to cowardice. For the sake of my own mental peace, I didn't rein in my wife when her behaviour had become intolerable, and a poor girl, an unborn baby, and my own son were ruined because of it.

'When you see something in front of you that you cannot agree with, Maharshi, take a stand against it. You saw what happened when I didn't.'

Bhogi then resumed the story.

14

The Beginning of the End or End of the Beginning

'A level of despair is reached, where people are willing to die to punish their tormentors.' – William Kammeraad-Campbell

Bhogi was slowly withdrawing from his active involvement in society. His elder son's divorce and remarriage had tainted his family's reputation and they were at a disadvantage when they started looking for a groom for their daughter Trupti. Finally, they were able to find a suitable boy from the Patidar clan. Kamlesh was an electrical engineer and had started his own company along with three of his college friends.

Slowly and steadily, Bhogi felt that life had started reassembling its broken pieces again. Kashyap had finished his medical school education and started his residency. He was very dynamic and had started getting leadership roles in his college while also developing relationships with the most important politicians in the state.

When Bhogi started noticing a repetition of complaints from Premila about Jatin's new wife Harsha, he realized his own folly in silently witnessing the harassment of his son's earlier wife. While he felt partly responsible for the divorce, the blot on his soul from knowing that an innocent baby had been murdered because he hadn't stop his wife from pursuing a campaign of hatred against their innocent daughter-in-law was dark.

With bitterness, Bhogi realized that he had taken on the role of Bhishma in his own household; someone who unwittingly facilitated and allowed evil to run its course by his own inaction. With trepidation, he remembered that Bhishma had paid for this with the loss of his entire family in conflict. Bhogi could only pray that karma was a little kinder to him than it was to Bhishma. But while he prayed with his heart, in his mind he knew that he would not be left unpunished for his sin of ignoring injustice.

In spite of all the petty politics, the family managed to live in a relative state of calm. With the start of Jatin's second married life and new job with a powerful government agency, however, all that began to change. Employment in his group gave immense powers to the hands of few engineers to permit or shut down any industry within their jurisdiction. With such power came the vulnerability to inducements at all levels. An engineer's role was to approve of factories for being within pollution-emitting guidelines. He was not answerable to any agency. Members of the office received substantial inducements from factory owners to ignore and overlook infringements on pollution guidelines.

After joining the agency, Jatin elected to join the herd. Some members also greatly enjoyed alcohol (despite Gujarat being a prohibition state) and were all too happy to induct a new member into their drinking club. Jatin was able to resist for a while but finally caved under peer pressure, gave in to the temptation and began to drink, play cards and live a more debauched lifestyle than anyone in his family.

At home, no one got to know. Jatin still played the devoted son to his parents, listened to what they told him, performed his duties as a brother, and seemed none the worse for wear. The only difference was that he often returned home late from work and went straight to his room, locking it, ostensibly to finish his work in peace. Being the trusting father he was, Bhogi never had any idea of what was happening.

One day, Premila's servant didn't arrive on time. So she decided to clean Jatin's room herself. She noticed that his shelves were full of dust and proceeded to wipe them. While doing so, she moved aside some books on the shelf and found a bottle of Johnny Walker hidden behind them. Premila had never touched or even been in close proximity of alcohol before. She had no idea what the bottle contained and, out of curiosity, showed it to Bhogi that evening.

'Look what I found in Jatin's room. Do you know what it is?'

Not nearly as innocent as his wife, Bhogi was able to identify the contents of the bottle the moment she brought it to his attention. 'It's a bottle of whisky.'

Bhogi was heartbroken. In his mind and to his generation, alcohol was one of the foremost evils that plagued man. In the village, the only ones who consumed alcohol were the worst of the lazy and spoiled zamindars, who earned money by living off the labour of others, and the lowest classes of society. Alcohol had a fiercely negative connotation as only those who were amoral or were failures in life consumed it in his day and age. He himself had never touched it, nor had any others in his family up to that point.

Bhogi broke down in tears. The bottle of alcohol was a symbol that he had failed in his duty as a father. He was too sad to even deal with his son when Jatin got home. He decided that anger would not be the proper solution to deal with the issue. He took Kashyap into confidence.

Kashyap was emphatic: 'This is ridiculous. We cannot allow this kind of clandestine behaviour in our family. He knows it displeases you; else he wouldn't have hidden it.'

Kashyap immediately wanted to confront Jatin and forcibly stop the covert alcohol consumption. He was restrained by his father, who felt that as Jatin was a grown man such a course would result in driving him away from the family. After much argument, Kashyap agreed to go along with Bhogi's plan. They talked to Jatin lovingly and rationally. They tried their best to stop him from drinking, but he simply wouldn't listen to them.

'I am a grown man,' Jatin argued. 'I can enjoy the occasional drink without suffering any ill-effect. Mind your own business; I can handle it just fine.'

Jatin continued to have drinks with his colleagues the moment his work ended at the office. As factory owners realized this, they brought him premium Scotches along with their bribes to make them more attractive, which only served to worsen his habit.

After having led a peaceful life, Bhogi was now cursed by this addiction of his son. Even so, the alcoholism hadn't reached a point where it posed problems for the quality of their family life. On his part, Jatin was an extremely nice man and despite the occasional bouts of anger, he was still dependable. One day, however, the downside of alcohol became clear.

Jatin was on a business trip. Along with three other officers from his board, he had to travel to a factory on the border of Gujarat. It was a five-hour car journey on very shabby roads. On the way back, one of the officers brought out a bottle of Scotch, and all of them, including the driver, began drinking. In their alcohol-induced mood, they had an absolute blast, that is, until the driver misjudged a turn and flipped the car upside down at 90km per hour.

All the occupants were severely injured, though none fatally. Jatin spent the next two months on a hospital bed. He was released after countless surgeries, and a slight limp to remind him of his troubles. His right ankle had a permanent deformity and prolonged immobilization in the plaster cast had led to partial paralysis of his right foot.

Bhogi went to the hospital and spoke to his son. 'Now can you see where your drinking has got you?'

Kashyap added, 'You're lucky to be alive – you do know that, right? With your injuries you could well have died.'

Jatin meekly remarked that it wouldn't happen again.

A saying in India goes that there are three types of people: the intelligent ones that learn from the mistakes of others, the average ones that learn from their own mistakes, and the fools that don't learn from either. Despite all his talents and intellect, Jatin resumed drinking after a mere three-month hiatus, which solidly landed him a place in the third category.

The situation reached breaking point one night when he was alone in the office. No one knows exactly when or how it began but in the late 1990s, Jatin started an affair with a Muslim secretary. At first it appeared to be a temporary fling, but it developed into an alternate depraved existence that soon began to interfere with his regular life.

Sparks began to fly at home when, from reports of concerned friends from Jatin's office, the family learnt of the affair. At first Jatin vehemently denied it but then switched to a defence mechanism, trying to minimize the implications of the affair. The family, however, didn't see it that way. Not used to being criticized for his actions, Jatin pointedly ignored their advice as the fights became more frequent.

His behaviour also deteriorated. There were several nights when Jatin returned home drunk out of his mind, stumbling across the hallway to his bedroom while waking up everyone else. Bhogi had never had to deal with something like this and was utterly draconian in his pronouncement that Jatin would have to totally stop drinking. His second biggest mistake was that, rather than acknowledging that his son had an addiction problem which needed to be treated, Bhogi viewed it as a demon that could only be excised by immediate removal.

This continued for years, with the number of drunken nights and arguments until the wee hours of the morning were steadily increasing. In the meanwhile, Jatin bought a newer and larger bungalow in the more rapidly developing side of the city. His family hoped that he had turned over a new leaf when, preoccupied with the building of the house, he cut down his alcohol consumption. Unfortunately, such was not the case, and a week after moving into the new house, Jatin picked up right back up from where he had left off.

Week by week, he seemed to enter a state of depression. Jatin claimed that there was a face on the ceiling fan of his bedroom, which frequently spoke to him and beckoned him. Despite no one else being able to see it, he insisted it was there. This reached a point where an exorcism was held in the house to remove the evil spirits. Following the ceremony, Jatin claimed the face disappeared.

Then, one evening, things really got out of hand. Jatin arrived home earlier, but more drunk than usual and began to brag about his Muslim 'acquaintance'. Seized as they were with shock, Bhogi, Premila and Harsha were unable to respond. At the height of his drunken arrogance, Jatin proclaimed that he would be bringing her home the next day and that she would live with them. This absurd notion snapped Bhogi out of his stupor and he responded with a firm and clear 'no', threatening to disown his son if he did such a thing. This sparked fury in Jatin, who began to curse at the top of his lungs. He uttered words that night that had never before been spoken in the calm house of Bhogi Mohanlal Patel. In shock and disgust, both Bhogi and Premila left the house to go to Kashyap's old home which had been empty since he had left for England with his wife Alpa and son Maharshi. Harsha didn't leave, however, and when she refused to be a part of Jatin's 'affair' charade, it incited him even further. With malevolence glinting in his crazed eye, as if he was possessed, Jatin slapped her hard across the face. Over the next hour, he beat his wife into near-unconsciousness until his son Ashutosh reached home. Silently, Ashutosh seized a cricket bat and forced Jatin out of the house.

He returned sobered up and repentant the next morning. Word of this reached Harsha's relatives who came the next morning, armed with knives, threatening that any further fingers laid on her would forfeit him of his life.

Bhogi's entire family denounced Jatin. All of them left the house that very day, living instead in Kashyap's old home. Two nights later Jatin, in the throes of guilt and depression, called them and his sister Trupti to his house, begging them to return. After being refused, he tried to swallow a bottle of poison. Kamlesh recognized the bottle for what it was and promptly tackled him to the ground, causing the bottle to fly out of his hands and break on the ground. As Kamlesh restrained him, Jatin tried to lick the spilled poison off the dirty floor, making for a gut-wrenching sight.

It was here that Bhogi made another blunder. Believing that it was a charade concocted by Jatin to gain his parents' compassion and forgiveness, he reiterated that until Jatin proved himself worthy of their love he was lost to all of them.

Trupti silently watched her brother go down a perilous path. She could not call Kashyap, now settled in the US, out of the simple fear that he would leave everything including his new practice and move back to India and it may still not serve the purpose. She and Kamlesh continually tried to rehabilitate Jatin back to his life.

A few weeks later Jatin again tried to bring his family, especially his two children whom he still loved, back to him. Bhogi, seeing the situation in black and white, refused again. Jatin begged his mother not to abandon him. She tearfully said that this decision was in Bhogi's hands.

The next morning, they received the worst phone call of their lives.

A young boy in Jatin's neighbourhood had an important exam coming up in a few weeks, and was studying late that night. He occasionally glanced out of his window, from where he was able to look inside Jatin's house. At around 3 in the morning he noticed that Jatin was walking in his bedroom with a towel on, looking like he had just showered. He also saw what looked like a bottle of whisky next to Jatin on the floor. Having heard rumours of the problems the family had undergone, the boy merely shook his head and went back to his desk and books. Then, at around 4, he heard what sounded like a muffled scream from the direction of Jatin's house. Expecting it to be some new drunken mischief he took the phone with him as he got up from his desk, prepared to call the police.

What he saw stunned him: Jatin was hanging limp and lifeless from the ceiling fan.. He had used his wife's dupatta as a noose to tie around his neck.

At that exact moment, Premila woke up hysterical from a nightmare she couldn't remember, except that Jatin's tortured face had appeared in it. 'My son is struggling to breathe!' she screamed. 'He is sinking. Please help him!' She started sobbing loudly.

Not knowing how to react, Bhogi downplayed her maternal instinct, 'Don't make any more noise. Let the neighbours sleep. We have been running around like crazed people for weeks on end because of your son's antics. Go back to sleep.'

'No, my Jatin is calling me. Please take me to Alok Bungalow. He is dying; he is choking . . . ' she cried.

Thinking that Premila would launch into hysteria if he didn't give in, Bhogi decided to go to Jatin's house. He reassured her and was getting dressed when the phone rang. It was his Kamlesh asking them to come to Alok Bungalow as something untoward had happened.

The police had arrived at the house minutes after the neighbours had called and, unable to establish contact with

Bhogi, they had called Trupti's home. Her husband had answered the phone and found out about what had happened. But he told his wife that there was an emergency at work and he had to leave.

Kamlesh went there immediately to identify the body, and was present when it was brought down from the fan. He decided to wait until morning to call the rest of the family there. When the first light of dawn illuminated the house Kamlesh called Bhogi and Trupti, telling them that there was an emergency and they would have to come to Jatin's house. Already suspecting something unnatural and evil afoot, Premila fainted at the news and Bhogi went alone.

When they arrived, Bhogi went into summary shock. Despite disowning his son, he harboured nothing but deep love for him. That he had been blinded by his hatred of Jatin's bad habits and had thus caused the situation to worsen became shockingly clear as he sobbed uncontrollably. His entire life had been devoted to ensure that his children would be better off than he had been and that when he died, he would know that his children were happy. Instead, he would be lighting his older son's funeral pyre.

Within the hour, Kamlesh called Kashyap in America. This was the first major setback in Maharshi's life. While his family was going through the most trying time in India, Kashyap had been left in the dark about recent events. He was hosting a party at his house at that time.

15

Teach a Man to Fish

'Almsgiving tends to perpetuate poverty; aid does away with it once and for all . . . Charity separates the rich from the poor; aid raises the needy and sets him on the same level with the rich.' – Eva Peron

Bhogi was devastated. He had been selected to watch as three generations of his family died before his eyes: his older brother, his father, his mother, his younger brother, his unborn grandchild and now his son.

The police called him later that day and asked him to come to the hospital so that he could identify the remains. Kamlesh offered to go but Bhogi insisted that he would go, alone.

Bhogi went by the same crowded bus he took everywhere since his retirement, despite having Jatin's car in his driveway and Kamlesh's offer for him to use his chauffeur and car. His destination was V.S. Hospital; ironically the same place where Kashyap had done his medical school internship.

Bhogi began to think.

The day that Jatin hanged himself from the blades of his bedroom fan was Bhogi's seventieth birthday. Every year from then onwards, instead of celebrating, Bhogi would have to mourn his son's death. No one could understand the burden of a father forced to light the pyre of his own son's body unless they had done it themselves. Bhogi had already had to cremate his father, mother and brothers. Now he was getting ready for what would be the hardest of all. This time he was going to light the flame that would burn his hopes, his desires and his sense of belonging to the world. Jatin's death marked the beginning of the end of Bhogi's attachment to anything worldly.

For Bhogi, life was nothing beyond a circus of death and drama. All these years he had devotedly read religious scriptures. He never touched alcohol. He had led the life an ascetic living in society. He never lied. He never cheated. He had avoided all possible sinful things in life. He always tried to remain non-judgemental and yet, fate had snatched away happiness at every stage of his life. His story was one long tale of trials and tribulations.

At the tender age of three years, he had witnessed death. His ears had heard the second chapter of the Bhagavad Gita that detailed the indestructible nature of the soul countless times. Yet, in real life when it struck and happened in front of him, he could never understand why he had to go through this so often. Each and every time he faced death, he thought: *This must be the last time I will have to go through this.* And just when he was ready to go on with his life, there was another ordeal waiting ahead of him to try and test his patience and his faith and trust in God. He finally truly understood Narsinh Mehta's final words.

'Bhalu Thayu, bhangi Janjal, Sukhe Bhajishu Shree Gopal'. Thank God, you relieved me of my bondages. Now I can worship you without any hindrances.'

Maybe it was time for Bhogi, like Narsinh Mehta, to finally denounce his attachments to the material world.

As the packed bus ride carried on, Bhogi contemplated about what he should do. He was tired. He envisioned a peaceful retirement in Hardwar where he could find solace in the remainder of his life, and leave behind the petty attachments and worries that life in a city invariably bring. He had been waiting for a time when he could wind up his worldly duties and move on to the Vanprastha Ashram on the banks of the Ganges, where he could spend the rest of his life like the Pandavas had, meditating until God finally accepted their souls to His abode.

Bhogi remembered the many dramas associated with Jatin's tortured last few years and shuddered. He realized with a jolt that life was more important than the petty arguments and useless machinations that had become a part of his family's daily interactions. He decided that enough was enough. Jatin had left behind more than enough money for his wife and children to live comfortably until they embarked on their own careers.

It was with this decision in mind that Bhogi walked into the hospital. Despite the pleasant weather outside, the waiting area was stifling. There were no fans, two measly wooden benches were already taken, and a huddle of family members of patients waited in the heat. The room stank with the odour of sweat that arises from many people cramped in a small space.

It was here that Bhogi had to wait for over three hours. When a young boy seated with his parents on one of the benches saw such an elderly man standing in the crowd, he waved at Bhogi. 'Dada, come here. Please take my seat.'

At first Bhogi said that he was OK, but the boy's parents saw what their chivalrous young son was trying to do and insisted that Bhogi take his seat.

After he sat, Bhogi asked, 'Is someone sick in your family?'

They responded, 'Yes bhaisaab, it is our daughter. She has suffered a bad accident. Her bicycle was struck by a fast car when she was on her way to school. We come to see her every day, but we have to wait here for at least three or four hours while her treatment is on.'

Bhogi offered his sympathies. As he watched, he noticed the young man in apparent discomfort. He asked, 'Son, are you feeling all right? You seem to be uncomfortable.'

'I'm fine, Dadaji; I'm just very hungry. I haven't had anything to eat since breakfast, but if we leave for food then we may miss the chance for me to see Didi.'

Bhogi realized that the hospital had no canteen. It was awful that in addition to the anxiety a patient's family goes through, they had to endure hunger while waiting in the hospital.

Finally Bhogi was taken to the morgue and asked if the body belonged to Jatin Patel. Before him was his son's lifeless body. The scars of the rope around his neck showed that he had struggled against the noose he himself had tied. Bhogi also saw the rudimentary job the coroner had done of sewing Jatin's body back together after the autopsy. The marks where the scalpel had torn open his chest were still visible. Bhogi almost fainted as he imagined his son's last moments, struggling against the hold of the dupatta after kicking the chair from under him, fighting for a few last gasps of precious air before the life was taken out of him. Overcome with sorrow, Bhogi nodded his head. He was told he could leave.

On his way back, Bhogi was even more overcome with grief than before. As he sat and thought, the words of the old man who had once rescued him from despair came back to him. 'Don't you think that by taking action and saving people's lives by building better roads, you will obtain thousands of times the satisfaction you get by ridiculing people's faith in God?'

The achievements he had predicted for Bhogi had indeed come true and Bhogi had been successful in preventing others from suffering his mother's fate. He also reflected over the countless sins his son had committed during his spiral downwards. He finally thought of the dead baby whose burden would be borne by him. Perhaps this was God's punishment to him.

What would happen to his family now? If he renounced life and moved to a hermitage, he was sure that his punishment would remain incomplete and would probably come down on his family instead. What was worse, his two grandchildren no longer had a father. Parthvi was yet to be married and Ashutosh was still in high school. Kashyap couldn't take care of them as he was in America. Bhogi's legacy was still alive in his grandchildren. He had to ensure that he saw them through life. To leave now would be tantamount to inflicting them with the same punishment that God had given him when Mohanlal left him. Thanks to his spartan lifestyle, he also had enough money to ensure their survival.

Bhogi's thoughts then turned to the poor boy worried about his sister while having to deal with the physical pain of hunger. He knew that this was a preventable suffering.

Bhogi then knew what his next calling in life would be.

God rewards those who work hard, he remembered. And He also rewards those who help others.

Since his retirement Bhogi hadn't done anything noteworthy. He had formed a Gurjeff study circle in the public garden where he and his retired friends assembled and read the texts of renowned philosophers like Ouspensky and Gurjeff. He and his wife had occasionally walked out in the winter to distribute blankets and slippers to homeless people sleeping on the footpath. He had inconsistently tried to share his own social duties. And yet, he hadn't tried to mediate in the many problems that had been occurring in his family, and hadn't done anything of significance for society beyond donating some money here and there.

On the crowded bus back home, Bhogi came to a decision. He wasn't going to escape into a sanctuary on the banks of the Ganges. He realized that doing so would not benefit the lives of others. On the other hand, if he stayed in Ahmedabad and volunteered to do social work, he could make an active difference in people's lives. He knew that the inner peace and satisfaction he would attain, knowing that he was doing something positive in society, would be much greater than what he would achieve through an entire lifetime spent meditating. He also believed that Jatin's children needed guidance and a good example of surviving against all odds in the face of calamity and death.

Bhogi went through a deep soul-searching. All his life he had everything snatched away from him. Although he was able to retain his worldly belongings, his priceless possessions had melted and dissolved in the eternal ocean of the cycle of birth and death. He was a mere witness to a melodrama that was playing out in front of his eyes. Every time he thought life had settled, it had gone upside down.

Slowly Bhogi realized the purpose of his life. The teachings of the Bhagavad Gita finally started making sense to him. Hadn't he read it over a thousand times? Hadn't Lord Krishna consoled Arjuna into not grieving for the dead as it is was a part of the eternal cycle of life and death? Wasn't it these verses that had inspired Gandhi to do such tremendous good in the world? He remembered those oft-spoken shlokas from the second chapter of the Bhagavad Gita:

Karmanye Va Adhikaraste Ma Faileshu Kadachan
Ma Karma Fal HeturBhu Ma Te Sangostva Akarmani

Yogastah Kurukarmani Sangamtyaktva Dhananjaya
SiddhiAsiddhi Samo Bhutva, Samatvam Yoga Uchyate

'You have the right to carry out selfless action alone and never to its fruits anytime. Never let the fruits be your motive for action. Never let there be attachment for inaction in you.'

It was with this in mind that Bhogi decided to set upon his first project. The hungry boy still hadn't left his mind. He called three retired friends, and told them his plan: 'I was at the hospital last week to identify Jatin's body. While I waited, I looked around and noticed so many people who had been made to wait for hours. They were anxious and also starving as they waited to see their loved ones. There isn't anything we can do to make the hospital more efficient, but we can at least alleviate people's suffering. Let's start a tiffin service.'

Bhogi's friends had nothing else to do with their time. They agreed to help him with his project. Each of them went around their individual neighbourhoods and asked their neighbours if they would prepare an extra meal a few times a week and donate it to their tiffin service for people waiting in the hospital. No one refused. Bhogi himself bought the metal containers for the meals. After the other elders pooled in their resources, they hired five servants who collected thirty tiffins each from the neighbourhood and brought them to the hospital to be given, at no cost, to the families in the waiting area.

Bhogi got busy organizing this service. Every now and then he accompanied the servants to the hospital and saw to it that everything ran smoothly. The first time he went, the staff behind the desk approached him so that they could meet 'the man behind the tiffin'.

'Bhaisaab,' they began, 'until now, we often had complaints about the condition in which people had to wait. The hospital barely has the money to keep itself functioning; it can't spare anything else. Despite the number of complaints we had, no one ever actually tried to make things better until you came along. Thank you.'

Those simple words moved Bhogi and he decided to devote the rest of his life in helping others in whatever way he could.

A few weeks after the project had begun, one of the servants fell ill. Bhogi decided to collect and deliver the tiffins himself. He took an autorickshaw – a luxury compared to the bus –to ensure that the food reached the hospital in time. As he handed out the tiffins, he noticed a group of seven poorly clad labourers huddled in the middle of the room. After serving the elderly individuals, he approached the group.

Bhogi asked them if they wanted the meal. One of the workers turned and said, 'Bhaisaab, we can barely afford to feed our families twice a day. We don't have the money to afford an extra meal for ourselves.'

Bhogi laughed and said, 'Come now, there is no charge for this. I'm just an old man trying to make the suffering of a loved one's hospital visit a bit easier.'

The labourers marvelled at this. Hesitantly, they accepted a tiffin and then immediately began to devour the food.

Bhogi soon came back to them and asked what brought them there. 'Sahib,' one of them explained, 'we all have come from Rajasthan in search of work. We arrived just two weeks back and found work to do the digging for a new set of underground power lines. Ramlal fell into one of the ditches and was struck by a live electric line. We brought him here, and are waiting to see how he is doing.'

Bhogi was struck by the devotion these poor individuals showed towards their friend. By leaving work to bring Ramlal to the hospital, they had forgone their daily wages and, in all likelihood, wouldn't be able to feed their families that night. Yet, when Bhogi offered them some money, they remonstrated with remarkable tenacity. 'Bhaisaab, we appreciate your generosity, but we cannot accept charity. We can still work and, for as long as our bodies can handle it, we will continue working to earn our sustenance.'

Bhogi was impressed by their strength and work ethic. He realized that a lot of wealthier people he knew, when faced with the pangs of hunger, would accept charity in a heartbeat. And here were people who faced that every day but refused to accept money that they felt they had not earned.

Bhogi was determined to help them. He asked them what was the biggest problem migrant workers faced. They responded that having arrived from tiny villages, food and basic groceries in the city were very expensive for them. Bhogi knew what he had to do.

He called together his friends and told them his plan. He wanted to start a food store that would exclusively cater to migrant workers. Every week, he would find a charitable vendor who would give him any amount of grains, rice or any grocery for a cheap price. He would then place these items for sale in a small store he would rent by the roadside near his neighbourhood. He would offer them for half the price at which he'd buy them. If a regular buyer fell short of money for any reason, he would be happy to offer the groceries for whatever price they could afford or even give them away for free.

As soon as Bhogi stopped talking, the negative responses began.

'It's absolutely impossible, I say. Vendors are too greedy to offer a good price.'

'Are you joking? Those good-for-nothing labourers will take complete advantage of you. You'll be finished in no time.'

Bhogi refused to listen to them. One of his friends, though, agreed to support him in his venture, and together they found a small place available for rent. Bhogi went and spoke to six vendors, and not a single one of them objected to his idea. One remarked that his father had first come to the city as a migrant worker; while he himself didn't have the time for charity work, he would be more than happy to help Bhogi. All the vendors agreed to sell Bhogi a given amount of grains and basic foodstuff for the same low price at which they had acquired them. The son of the migrant worker even agreed to give him any excess food he may receive for free.

Bhogi's faith in the basic goodness of man was already half affirmed. Many of his friends insisted that Bhogi alone should not bear the cost of selling grains at half the price he bought them for, so they all donated money to his initiative.

Bhogi set up his store and found a large clientele. To his surprise rarely did a worker tell him that he didn't have the money to buy the food that day, and requested it for free. The few times that they didn't have the money, Bhogi did give it for free without asking for any explanation. But they always returned the next day and paid him the due amount.

One day, a member of the group of the seven men at the hospital came to Bhogi's store. When he saw Bhogi, he immediately recognized him. He went back to his co-workers and told them, 'Come and see what Tiffin Dada has done now!'

All seven, accompanied by a now-recovered Ramlal, went to the store. When Bhogi explained that what they had told him that day inspired him to open the store, every one of them blinked back tears and thanked him for his sacrificing and charitable spirit. Their kind words brought Bhogi to tears himself.

In this manner, Bhogi's faith was proven to be well founded. He realized that he had done the world a much bigger service by his volunteer work than he ever could have by renouncing it for a lonely ashram and embracing meditation.

In the next six years Ashutosh, Bhogi's grandson, completed his medical studies from the same college that Kashyap had attended. His granddaughter Parthvi went on to work for a BPO firm after graduation. Bhogi continued to live the life of a karma yogi, surviving on barely $300 a month including food for the entire family. While the family feud had ended long ago, fights between Premila and Jatin's widow Harsha still took place off and on. Bhogi continued to serve the landless and homeless labourers coming to the city in search for employment.

As the days passed, the family slowly came out of mourning and began to live life anew. With the death of her son, Premila finally realized exactly how much her possessiveness for her son, an unnatural maternal feeling, had harmed them. She was face to face with the realization that she had created the monster that had ripped them apart. She no longer played the role of the vicious mother-in-law; instead, she decided to be more constructive.

Premila almost stopped talking entirely and devoted her energy to prayer and helping temples. Every morning she woke up at 5.30 for early-morning prayers, and slowly washed the taint of selfishness off. She eventually also reconciled with her daughter-in-law. Bhogi Mohanlal Patel's house finally became the peaceful and quiet home that he had always wanted it to be. Along with her husband, Premila also started dedicating her time and life to the cause of helping others. The day the delivery man did not show up, she went from house to house to collect tiffins and deliver them to the hospital. Her life was now devoted to God.

16

Resurgence

'Do not be proud of wealth, people, relations and friends, or youth. All these are snatched by time in the blink of an eye. Give up this illusory world, know and attain the Supreme.' – Adi Shankaracharya

It was with this that Bhogi ended his story, and looked at a spellbound Maharshi. 'My dear son,' he said, 'can you see now why I am able to be content with so little and be happy despite having seen such troubles?'

Maharshi confessed that while he was enthralled by the story, he couldn't explain why Bhogi was happy and content.

'Well, let me ask you this then,' his grandfather continued. 'Do you know why you are unhappy despite the vast amounts of resources you have at your command? Everything you've ever done has been pursuing the end of your own pleasure. You freely spend money on things that satisfy you. What good does an expensive car do? A car's purpose is to get you from one place to another, but you bought a $60,000 car because you wanted people to notice you along the way. You perverted the purpose of a necessity to suit your own pride. Similarly, you eat meals that cost $40 or $50. The purpose of food is basic sustenance, and I can achieve that for a month for less than half of what you spend on one meal.

'I can divine one major reason for your unhappiness. Everything you've done in your life has been to the end of getting recognition from others. You wear expensive clothes because others will see them and think that you are wealthy. You drive an expensive car because it will get you noticed. You place the value of your self-worth on what others will think of you. For as long as you do this, even if you achieve all the material success in the world, you will still not be happy.

'Your father told me what you were like when you were young. You were always honest, always moral. Ever since your father became wealthy, you started hiding away from your true self. You began indulging in shallow talks that created a gap between your true self and what you projected yourself to be. As time went by you, you almost developed a fear of confronting what your projection had ended up becoming. That's why you paid money to keep your ego boosted by bartenders or tuxedo-clad hosts in expensive restaurants. You thought that by paying exorbitant amounts of money, you could buy artificial happiness and acceptance.

'This morning, you went to Tushar Mama's house to take a shower and get ready. Why?'

'Tushar Mama's house has the best amenities,' Maharshi automatically replied. 'His house has running hot water. It's as close as I can get to being back home.'

'And how long did you take in the shower?'

'About half an hour.'

'Why so long?'

'Well, a long shower always helps me relax and handle stress better.'

Bhogi shook his head and said, 'That may be true, but do you know how it helps you do that? You spend more time showering not because it is comfortable but because the feeling of warm water soaking your body takes you away from that which is stressing you, and you want to stay away from your problems for as long as possible. It is once again escapism from facing the problems that arose when your true self and the self you portrayed weren't in congruence. Everything you have done in your life has contributed to this escapism. Video games, movies, long showers – all are means to that end. Instead, you should have tried to confront what is stressing you and remove the stress rather than mask its symptoms by escaping.

'I am not a perfect man by any means. I too made the mistake of escapism. When there was a conflict in my house, rather than facing the unfortunate situation and doing something about it, I escaped. While you escaped to luxury cars, restaurants and parties, I dived into work and solitude. I had the readymade excuse of my brother's death: no one would have blamed me for not becoming involved. But my escapism led to the death of an unborn baby, the ruin of an innocent daughter-in-law and the suicide of my oldest son.'

'How can I get back on the right path and bring out the person I really am, Dada?' Maharshi asked in response, realizing the truth in everything his grandfather was saying.

'Well, the first thing you need to do is to start accepting yourself for who you really are. From what your father has told me, I know that you always felt bad when you were young because you didn't really have many friends. Yet, you were true to yourself. Somewhere along the line you associated being true to yourself with being a loner which is wrong, utterly wrong. You had friends in your ninth and tenth grade, before you were rich. You need everything in moderation. Is having a pack of friends really worth the pain you suffered as your actions became more and more out of line with the person you really were? You need to realize that the friends you gained because they thought that you were someone you weren't, aren't real friends. Once you accept this, you will stick to who you really are: the kind, sweet, moral boy whom his father used to call Little Gandhi. The arrogant brat you pretended to be will fade into nothingness. Slowly, the schism between your true self and what you want to be will start disappearing.

'You had asked why even slum dwellers in India have a look of contentment on their faces. To answer that, I will tell you something that Gandhi once proclaimed. Only he whose thoughts, beliefs and actions are totally in line with each other will truly be happy. That, Son, is why they are happy and why you are not. They never pretend to be people they aren't. Being content with oneself transcends race, religion social and economic boundaries.

'Once you start finding peace between yourself and your surroundings, your ability to accept people and circumstances will enhance. You will slowly stop being critical or judgemental about others. You will learn to live in complete harmony with nature which, to me, is the whole purpose of creation. It is to allow all forms of life to live in harmony with each other – something your Western scientists refer to as symbiosis.

'I will give you one final reason why I am so content. The work that I do now helps others. The satisfaction that you will receive by helping even one person is more than you will ever get from the flattery and admiration of hundreds.'

Maharshi wryly smiled. 'Oh come on, Dada. Do you really think that your actions will make a real difference to the poverty and injustice in this world? It's like you're sitting on the edge of an ocean and taking water out spoon by spoon, convinced that you are slowly reducing its volume when actually it's fruitless.'

Bhogi shook his head again 'The best answer that I can give you is one I actually got from a story I once read in your Western literature. It describes a man who was walking along a beach and saw another man further down. He was picking up starfish that had been brought to the shore by the tide and was throwing them back into the sea. The man went up to him and asked him what he was doing. "Well, if the starfish don't go back into the ocean, they will die. I am saving their lives," he responded. The first man, who was like you, shook his head and said, "But there are countless starfish along the beach. What difference will throwing in a few make?" The other man responded by throwing another starfish into the water and saying, "Well, it made all the difference in the world to that one."

'Gandhi himself said, "The difference between what we do and what we are capable of doing would suffice to solve most of the world's problems. Almost everything you do will seem insignificant, but it is important that you do it."

'The Ancient Egyptians believed that when you die, you are taken before the gates of heaven and asked two questions that would sum up the most important aspects of your life. Your answers would determine if you were permitted entrance. The first question is, "Have you experienced joy in your life?" And the second: "Has your life brought joy to others?". For myself, I think that I can comfortably answer yes to both.

'So you see, Son, my secret to happiness arises out of the fact that I have managed to let go of everything that ties me to the world. What I profess to be and what I really am are in line. I have embraced the fact that every man is born on this earth to die one day and that nothing we do can change that truth. However, what we can do is make a change in the world, so that each day becomes better.'

Maharshi finally realized that his search for inspiration had ended with his grandfather. He was sure that there were many Bhogi Mohanlal Patels in the world, who lived silent lives of service to humanity without any expectation of rewards or the desire to leave behind their mark. He understood the difference between wealth and happiness, between being true to himself and maintaining facades. He was literally bowled over.

'Let me finish by quoting a famous aphorism from the Ishavasya Upanishad,' Bhogi then said.

'Isha vasyam idam sarvam, yatkimcha jagatyam jagat. Ten tyakten bhunjitha, ma gridhah kasya swid dhanam.'

'Dada, you know that I can't understand Sanskrit. What does that quote mean?' Maharshi curiously asked.

'Maharshi Beta, this is much more than a quote. This philosophy has kept Hinduism alive for over 5000 years. Many religions have come and gone and perished in the meanwhile, but ours has always been there. The verse means "This whole universe and every form of creation in nature is fully pervaded by the Almighty God. Enjoy and utilize your all justified wealth and prosperity which is yours in accordance with your practice of righteousness."

'It means, Son, that you renounce all that is not a necessity and enjoy it all the more so by renunciation. That is what pure delight truly is. Not in the lavish spending of money on yourself, but on spreading it to help promote righteousness in the world. Do not use more than you need, for you are depriving others by doing so. Remember, Gandhi also said, "There is enough on this earth to satisfy every man's needs, but not every man's greed."

'Beta, you know this was the foundation of Gandhiji's philosophy. He said we all are the trustees of God's creation. We should only draw out our own necessities and renounce everything else. It was with this simple philosophy that he was able to defeat the entire British empire without shedding a drop of blood.

'Go on, my son. Go and be successful. Enjoy the fruits of wherever life takes you, but always remember those words.'

17

A New Beginning

'What we call the beginning is often the end. And to make an end is to make a beginning. The end is where we start from.' – T.S. Eliot

As Bhogi's story ended, Maharshi began to wonder what he would do now. Rather than disown him and force him to face his demons alone, his parents had promised to support him in whatever way they could. His father optimistically believed that no matter what, everything that happened in the world happened for the best. According to Kashyap, the experiences of real life were greater than anything that can be learned from books.

On their flight to India Kashyap had shared his own story, of his optimism that had led him to America, the country that had allowed him to make his fortune.

When Kashyap was in India, fresh out of his fellowship training at a prestigious institution in Bombay, he was promised a job at a hospital in Ahmedabad by the dean of the public medical school. He would be an assistant professor of haematology there. Kashyap had an advantage in that he had been able to cultivate connections with the most powerful politicians and businessmen in the city. The job that he was promised was not in existence then, and being a public medical college, the approval of state politicians was required. Using his political clout, Kashyap had the post created. The dean, however, appointed the son of his best friend. Kashyap had been used by the dean to get the position created, and then he lost the post to nepotism.

Kashyap was quite disappointed, but he had to take up a job at a less reputable medical school. While there, he met a devoted nephrologist who had been trained in the UK. He encouraged Kashyap to pursue research and further training abroad, particularly in England. Kashyap applied to over 400 hospitals across the world so that he could acquire additional training in cancer. Of them, only one responded positively.

Destiny took Kashyap to north-west England in 1992. Within months, Maharshi and Alpa joined him. They lived in a one-bedroom hospital dorm, sharing a lounge and kitchen with other doctors.

While Kashyap had been pursuing his career, his wife gave up an immensely promising and lucrative career as an attorney in India to stand by her husband's side in England and raise Maharshi. It was a hard life. Kashyap changed hospitals every six months, and they had to move six times across England and Scotland in the time span of four years.

Persistent and relentless efforts enabled Kashyap to migrate to the US, where local regulations forced him to redo six years of residency and fellowship that he had already completed in India and England. He finished in 2002 and they finally had a permanent home in Charlotte. Maharshi knew the rest of the story.

One thing that Maharshi observed in his dad's story was that he was an eternal optimist and saw that there were never any permanent calamities or tragedies. They were only changes in circumstances and that something good always came out of the so-called difficulties, provided that people had the patience to wait long enough.

If that dean had not taken Kashyap for a ride at the start of his career, Maharshi's story would never have developed or evolved the way it did. Kashyap was confident that Maharshi's journey back to his roots in India would be beneficial in the long run.

He was right. Bhogi's tale was now in its twilight hours, but Maharshi's story had barely begun. Bhogi gave Maharshi the greatest gift that he could possibly have; a gift that went far beyond anything that money could ever buy. He gave his grandson the gift of wisdom that could only be accrued from a lifetime of hardship and experience.

It was with this wisdom that Maharshi took the next step forward in his life. He recognized the truth that was behind his grandfather's words and was determined to no longer live a life that was exclusively focused on the gain of material goods for himself. He would be the eagle; not the lion. He would begin living a life based on necessities; not on lavish and wasteful desires.

For the next six months, Maharshi set aside ambition and material gain for the sake of work that truly made a difference in the lives of others. He took up an unpaid fellowship with Sarvajal, an organization that had been created to provide rural villagers with the basic necessity of clean and affordable drinking water. Just like Bhogi had suggested, Maharshi began to reduce his needs. Turning down the use of one of his family's cars, he instead travelled by autorickshaw every morning and evening. He worked in a non air-conditioned office even during the sweltering Indian summer.

Through his work with Sarvajal, Maharshi often visited various villages around Gujarat that had company purifiers installed. He met men and women there who still lived like his grandfather once had. In the villages, he saw people with few amenities. They still commuted by camel or bullock cart. As Maharshi watched a bullock cart carrying purified water for home delivery down a dusty road one day, he visualized the dark and cold night, Bhogi crying seated in the rear and being comforted by Hari as the cart hastened to reach his deceased father. He met many others who were highly reminiscent of the long-departed characters of Bhogi's story.

On his visit to Vasai, on the slopes of Mount Ider, Maharshi spoke to some villagers who had come to collect the purified water. The water in the village was severely contaminated by the fluoride from mountain rocks. Almost the entire adult population of Vasai suffered steadily worsening arthritis and joint pains, manifestations of skeletal fluorosis brought on by constant consumption of fluoride from dirty drinking water. Maharshi talked in the broken Gujarati typical of people who had left the country when they were young. He began a conversation with a very frail-looking lady. He could tell that she appeared a little nervous about talking to someone who had just stepped out of a company car with a notepad and pen in hand. He thus tried to put her at ease.

'Aunty, how are you?' Maharshi respectfully asked.

'I'm fine, Son.'

'Would it be all right if I asked you a few questions while you wait for your water?'

'It would be fine.'

'I work for Sarvajal, and I wanted to talk to some people from around the village. Would you like some tea?' Maharshi put away his notebook and pen. The woman then felt comfortable and assented. They went to the nearby tea shop where Maharshi ordered two steaming cups of masala chai.

'I want to see the sort of background our customers come from. Could you tell me your name?'

'Certainly. My name is Kashi.'

Maharshi gave her a rather odd look and asked, 'Could you tell me a little about your family?'

'Well, Son, I am thirty-three years old. I lost my husband to tuberculosis five years ago and have been taking care of our two children since. I have a six-year-old son, Shiv, and a seven-year-old daughter, Pyaari.'

The similarity to the Kashi of his own lineage unnerved Maharshi. He asked the woman whether she bought clean water for the sake of her health.

'Son, I honestly don't worry about my health any more. My life is solely for my two kids now. I don't want them to get sick. I buy it for my children to have a long and healthy life.'

As she spoke, Maharshi felt that his own great-grandmother must have been a lot like this woman. While this lady walked for almost a mile each morning to fill 10 litres of pure water for her children's health, Kashi bent over for hours every morning picking apart kalas for cotton so that her children could survive.

Finally, Maharshi asked if this drinking water had helped. To his surprise, the woman said that the almost crippling joint pains she had suffered for the past few years had reduced ever since she started drinking clean water. It appeared that her skeletal fluorosis was getting better.

Maharshi was elated. He hadn't felt like this in many years. Here, in front of him, was someone whose life he had made tangibly better as a result of the work he was doing. The satisfaction that he felt at that moment was infinitely greater than that he had ever received from compliments about his car and his clothes. He finally understood the satisfaction that the man throwing starfish into the ocean got after each life that he saved. He finally understood the axiom that Gandhi had lived by – that by helping others he could help himself. The reason why even labourers could be more at ease with life than the wealthiest of the wealthy.

As Maharshi was about to get up and leave, the woman stopped him.

'Son, why don't you tell me a little about yourself? It is clear that you aren't from here.'

Maharshi chuckled. 'Actually I am from this area. I was born in India twenty years ago. My entire family has been in Gujarat for generations. My grandfather lived in a village even smaller than this one. But when I was still very young, I left for abroad. I lived in England and America. But now, I'm back.'

Kashi's eyes grew in wonder. 'But why would anyone come back from those countries? It must have been wonderful there. What brought you back here?'

Maharshi laughed again. 'Aunty, those countries are far from wonderful. It is true that I had more material comforts there. The houses were bigger, the cars were faster, the money was flowing, and I was drawn right in by it. But I realized that I was miserable. It changed the person I was, and I wasn't happy. I came back to India entirely lost, and it was my village-raised grandfather who got me back on track.'

As he spoke, Maharshi remembered all of Bhogi's words and advice to him. 'I realized that my actions and my heart weren't in line. My behaviour wasn't suited to the man I had been raised to become. I ignored it for a while, but it made me miserable. It took a trip back to this country, back to my roots, to see where I had fallen off. I was behaving without regard to others, without considering just how wasteful my actions were. But here, I realized that money doesn't bring happiness; being true to yourself does.'

Maharshi also remembered Einstein's story, about how evil wasn't God's creation but a result of the absence of love and empathy in people's hearts. He realized that he had been working in the blazing heat of the Indian summer in a non-air-conditioned office. He had been the avoiding almost all the luxuries he once thought he could never live without. Where did all this strength come from?

Maharshi suddenly recalled the story of the man who had once spoken to Vivekanand. He realized that the strength for enduring a harsher life came from within, from the awareness that he was doing good work that would help countless numbers of people. He also knew that as long as he did things that helped others in addition to himself, God would always ensure that he would be content and able to achieve his goals. He finally understood why Bhogi lived the way he lived.

In front of Maharshi was a lady, the namesake of Kashi, who was making the same sacrifices his great-grandmother had once made. He had come full circle, back to where his lineage had begun. Back home.

Here, Maharshi didn't have a Mercedes. He no longer wore Lacoste shirts. He didn't party every other night. Yet here, in India, where Bhogi's story had begun over seventy years ago, Maharshi was finally happy.

Acknowledgements

Without the help, guidance, and friendship of a number of people, this book would never have come to fruition.

I first have to thank my parents, Kashyap and Alpa, who moulded me into who I am today. I have to thank my aunts and uncles, Tushar Mama, Prity Mami, Prajay Mama, Pinki Mami, Kamlesh Fua, Trupti Bua, and Harsha Auntie, for their love, affection, and patience with me, and my cousins Arya, Shyam, Parthvi and Asutosh for never failing to bring a smile to my lips. I have to also thank Dr Julie Nathwani for introducing me to the literary world. I also want to thank Vijay Uncle and especially Swati Auntie, for being friends as close as family and for all of their help, kindness, emotional support, and Swati Auntie's delicious desserts.

I want to thank Dean Stephen Bryan and Dean Sabrina Thomas from Duke University; two people who were great inspirations and the key instrumentals for rebuilding my hopes, dreams, and ambitions.

I owe special thanks to the peerless and lovely author Shobhaa De, who was the Drona to my Arjun through the writing process. I also owe special thanks to family friend Harkin Chatlani, who selflessly spent time and effort in guiding me through the unfamiliar channels of the publishing world.

I want to thank Jitu Dada, Premi Ba, and Jyoti Ba (who I know is lovingly watching over me from the Beyond) for the blind and unconditional love that only a grandparent can have. Finally, I want to thank Bhogi Dada, for his love, support, guidance, and especially the inspiration you have seen in the pages.